❧ SOCIETY WEDDINGS ❧

Together with their families

Clio Norwood
and
Stefan Bianco

invite you to join them as they become

Mr. & Mrs.

June
Two Thousand Fifteen

The Chatsfield
New York, New York

Reception to follow

**...but only if Stefan
can claim his unexpected bride!**

❧ SOCIETY WEDDINGS ❧

Dedicated bachelors Rocco Mondelli, Christian Markos, Stefan Bianco and Zayed Al Afzal met and bonded at university, wreaking havoc among the female population. In the decade since graduating they've made their marks on the worlds of business and pleasure, becoming wealthy and powerful.

Marriage was never something Rocco, Christian, Stefan or Zayed were ever after...but things change, and now they'll have to do whatever it takes to get themselves to the church on time!

Yet nothing is as easy as it seems... and the women these four have set their sights on have plans of their own!

Your embossed invitation is in the mail and you are cordially invited to:

The marriage of *Rocco Mondelli & Olivia Fitzgerald*
April 2015

The marriage of *Christian Markos & Alessandra Mondelli*
May 2015

The marriage of *Stefan Bianco & Clio Norwood*
June 2015

The marriage of *Sheikh Zayed Al Afzal & Princess Nadia Amani*
July 2015

So RSVP and get ready to enjoy the pinnacle of luxury and opulence as the world's sexiest billionaires finally say "I do"...

Tara Pammi

The Sicilian's Surprise Wife

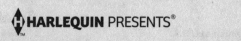

ISBN-13: 978-0-373-13345-1

The Sicilian's Surprise Wife

First North American publication 2015

Copyright © 2015 by Harlequin Books S.A.

PLEASE RECYCLE
THIS PRODUCT IS RECYCLABLE

Recycling programs
for this product may
not exist in your area.

Special thanks and acknowledgment are given to Tara Pammi
for her contribution to the Society Weddings series.

Printed in U.S.A.

www.Harlequin.com

Tara Pammi can't remember a moment when she wasn't lost in a book, especially a romance, which was much more exciting than a mathematics textbook. Years later, Tara's wild imagination and love for the written word revealed what she really wanted to do. Now she pairs alpha males who think they know everything with strong women who knock that theory and them off their feet!

Books by Tara Pammi

Harlequin Presents

The Man to Be Reckoned With
A Deal with Demakis

A Dynasty of Sand and Scandal
The Last Prince of Dahaar
The True King of Dahaar

The Sensational Stanton Sisters
A Hint of Scandal
A Touch of Temptation

Visit the Author Profile page
at Harlequin.com for more titles.

For the three wonderful ladies
who made working on this book such a treat—
Andie, Jen and Michelle.

CHAPTER ONE

She felt like glass, stretched so tightly that a gentle tap could shatter her forever.

Clutching her wrap tight in her fingers, Clio Norwood looked around for her fiancé, Jackson.

Ashley, his secretary, who had arrived unannounced and interrupted their meeting with a client Jackson was determined to add to his cap, was nowhere to be seen either. Something distasteful hovered in the back of Clio's mind, as if waiting to strike.

With the small get-together of the ultrarich in full swing atop the Empire State Building, Manhattan glittered around them.

Usually, the vibrant, unrelenting pulse of the city that had become home to Clio over the past decade filled her with unending spirit for life. It had kept her going even when she had been struggling after graduation from Columbia University. And had helped her swallow her failures and her naive, broken expectations of making it by herself in the city that never slept.

But tonight, even New York couldn't puncture the bubble of dread that had begun to pervade her of late.

Jackson had returned last night after three weeks from an overseas trip and had been in *a stinker of a mood* as he liked to call it, because he had missed out on some real estate deal.

They had barely exchanged a word all day today as she

had been at work. When she had returned to the posh flat
they had been living in for the past year, he had commanded
her to get ready for this party tonight.

Commanded and not asked, much less requested. A pattern that was becoming more and more obvious to Clio.
Still, she knew the stress of his business, understood the
driving need to make one's mark in the world, so she had
given in.

Even if she was still bone tired from the out-of-season
flu she had had a week ago.

Tonight, Jackson needed her help to convince Mrs. Alcott, an old friend of her parents', to hire him as her personal investment banker. With her estates in Britain and
substantial family business, Jane Alcott would be a coup
for Jackson's already flourishing career.

But they hadn't even greeted Jane properly before Ashley had approached Jackson with a desperate glint in her
eye.

Loath to create a scene, Clio had clenched her teeth
and smiled serenely even as she saw the curious looks and
stifled whispers among Jackson's clients' wives and girlfriends. Even the utter kindness of Jane's question if everything was all right between Jackson and her had been
unbearable.

*What was going on with him? What was going on be-
tween them?*

Because Clio knew with a nauseating clarity that Ashley was just the tip of the iceberg for what was going on
between her and Jackson.

Suddenly, it felt blatantly scandalous of Ashley to drag
him away with a barely disguised proprietary claim on him.

Squaring her shoulders, Clio let her long stride eat up
the space. She hated creating a scene, hated the pitying
and speculative glances that had been coming her way far
too frequently the past few months, but she had endured it
all silently.

Tonight, she had had enough. She stilled as a tall, commanding figure came into her focus.

Clio blinked, the impact of those jade green eyes and generous but scornful mouth instantaneous.

Stefan Bianco.

Her first instinct was to head for the elevator before he could see her, leave the party. Even her parents, with their disapprovingly stifling silence, would have been welcome. She didn't want the man she had known a long time ago, one of her oldest friends, to see her tonight.

Stefan, Christian, Rocco and Zayed made up the Columbia Four—the four young men she had known when they had all been at university together, who had turned into supersuccessful, ultrawealthy, sought-after bachelors for whom the world was a playground and its most beautiful women were playthings.

But before they had all become successful in their own right, she had known them, had seen them every day for four years, and had shared her deepest fears and hopes with them.

And the fact that she wanted to run away from one of the few people who had genuinely known her, had understood her, left a bitter taste in her mouth.

Was she that much of a failure, then? Was she running away from Stefan or was she running away from what she had become?

Stefan Bianco looked around at the glittering cityscape of Manhattan and gritted his jaw tight.

The vibrant pulse of it, the memories from almost a decade ago everywhere he looked, his own sheer naïveté when he had studied at Columbia with his other three friends—the memories rose up around him like a specter that wouldn't let him breathe easy even for a few minutes.

And yet, as the head of a multimillion luxury real estate

company, New York was unavoidable even though he tried to reduce the number of times he came here.

But this time, he had a reason for being at this exact party, on top of the Empire State Building.

It was high time he found a way to stop Jackson Smith.

The memory of his executive assistant Marco's whitened face as he lay against the hospital bed after his suicide attempt, Marco's five-year-old daughter's chubby face wreathed in confusion as she asked Stefan about what had happened to her papa…

The powerlessness he had felt was like acid in his stomach.

Jackson had swindled Marco out of his savings, pushed him to bankruptcy, until his assistant had lost everything, had seen no way out…

The eviscerating self-doubt, the sense of being an utter failure, of letting down everyone that had counted on him— looking into Marco's eyes had been like looking at his own reflection of a few years ago.

Guilt corroded his insides. If only he had found a way to stop Jackson years ago when he had swindled Stefan himself…

It had been the worst time of his life—Serena's betrayal, his guilt driving him to not return to his parents in Sicily and the around-the-clock hours he had worked to secure a deal…

He had lost the little he had made because of Jackson's treachery. He would have been in Marco's place if it hadn't been for his friends Rocco, Christian and Zayed anchoring him, if he hadn't already been woken up to the reality of life by Serena, the woman who had professed to love him.

This time Jackson needed to be stopped, whatever it took.

As though Stefan thinking Jackson's name invoked the very devil himself, the American laughed in a group not two feet from where Stefan stood.

A short blonde, dressed in jeans and a tight T-shirt, dragged Jackson away, interrupting the conversation. His craggy face tight with tension, Jackson leaned toward another woman in the group, a tall redhead, and whispered something.

An apology, Stefan assumed. That didn't quite work, given the way the woman flinched and turned her head away. More curious than ever, Stefan looked on as the woman's bare shoulders stiffened, bones jutting out of her shoulders.

Everything about her posture screamed tension and something more. Jackson let himself be dragged away even as the tall woman stood ramrod straight, her head held high and so perfectly still that Stefan wondered if she would break if someone blew a wisp of breath her way.

Her face wreathed in shadows, there was a quiet dignity to her. And then he noticed her hair. Even tucked away from that angular face and scrunched tight into an elaborate knot, that red hair was as unmistakable as the narrow, upturned nose and stubborn tilt of the chin.

That face would be perfectly oval and her eyes green, like glittering emeralds. When she smiled, one corner of her mouth turned upward in a crooked slant.

Clio Norwood, the one woman he had never tamed.

Every cell inside him went on high alert, as if he had been infused with a charge of live current. What the hell was Clio doing with Jackson Smith?

There had been intimacy in the way Jackson had bent closer to her and whispered something, in the way his open palm had caressed her bare arm.

Yet Stefan could feel the tension in her as the silence of the group reverberated against her. Saw the speculative and intrusively hungry glances cast her way. Noted the way she retreated into herself as an older woman inquired something.

And knowing Jackson and his perfidious ways, a thousand kinds of thoughts swarmed in on Stefan.

Anything even remotely connected to Jackson, Stefan didn't touch with a pole. Yet, he found himself moving toward her, his gaze savoring the sight of her. Inch by glorious inch, light bathed that long neck and her face.

He stilled, supremely aware of the insistent beat of his own pulse, of the heightened charge of his own breath.

Clio was just as utterly gorgeous as she had always been, if a little too thin.

His mind cast back to over a decade ago, to his university days with Rocco, Christian and Zayed—who'd become more brothers than friends—to the unparalleled enthusiasm of learning the world and knowing that it could be at their feet, to the glory of discovering women and the pull they held for them, and to Clio Norwood—the woman who had known the Columbia Four as well as they had known each other.

Every inch an aristocrat she no longer wanted to be and used to privileged playboys just like them, she had often laughed at their exploits, seeing their escapades with other women with a decidedly amused resignation and distance. She'd rejected his come-ons that first year, as easily as she had shrugged away the elaborate wealth and standing she had been born into.

Of all the men on the planet, the last man he would have envisioned Clio to be with was Jackson Smith.

In no mood to get into a sparring match with Jackson again, especially when his patience was already dangerously low, Stefan waited. Minutes piled on top of each other. With a graceful tilt of her head, Clio excused herself from the group.

Ignoring the uncharacteristically frantic thrumming of his heart, Stefan cornered her in the next moment. "*Ciao*, Clio."

He wrapped his fingers over her arm to turn her and felt the shiver that went through her. Saw the bracing breath she took before she turned around. A flash of fear, feral and bright, danced in her green eyes.

Until she blinked, those long lashes hiding her expression.

When she looked up again, a flicker of warmth dawned in those green depths. "Stefan...what a surprise...I had no idea you were in New York."

That accent of hers—it had always done strange things to his insides, swept over him with a mix of warmth and heated awareness. But her tone was reserved and artificial; it rattled him.

Granted, they hadn't seen each other in a while, but for four years, Clio had been a part of his life—an integral one and one he remembered without bitterness.

Placing his arm around her toward the railing, he trapped her, shielding her from the rest of the crowd.

"You would have known if you'd kept in touch, wouldn't you, *bella*?"

Tension thrummed in the tight set of her shoulders. "You barely ever set foot in New York whereas this is my home."

"True. But you didn't think it important to even attend Rocco's wedding. Does your new...*life* not allow room for old friends, Clio?"

She didn't flinch as she had done with Jackson, but there was an infinitesimal withdrawal. That shadow of fear again.

Dio, what was her association with Jackson?

"I've always been here, Stefan." A remnant of the old Clio—full of adventure and plans for a new kind of life—flashed in her gaze. "I'm not the one determined to wipe anything related to our life in New York from memory."

"Maybe I realized there wasn't anything of value left for me here in New York. It's not like Rocco, Christian or Zayed live here."

She didn't strike him down with words as she used to, only stared at him with those wide eyes and her mouth pinched. Why didn't she just put him in his place with a cutting remark as she had always done?

Where was this need to land a shot at her coming from?

And why? Just because she had some kind of association with Jackson Smith while she had rejected his cocky advances a lifetime ago?

He didn't need his male ego to be validated by her interest in him.

Women flocked to him with one interested glance from him and he took advantage of it. He liked sex, had a healthy libido and when he was done, he walked away from the woman whether she liked it or not.

He had no place or use for a woman in his life, except in his bed.

Yet he had barely spent two minutes with Clio and suddenly, he was more interested in her thoughts and her actions.

Her chest rose and fell with the calming breath she took, coating his skin with warmth. He saw the mask that fell into place covering up her obvious distress, saw years of breeding and good manners slide into place.

The very thing she had been determined to overcome about herself…

"It was good to see you, Stefan," she said evenly, with a perfectly bland smile. "But you'll have to excuse me. I have things to do."

He clasped her arm. "You didn't answer my question. Why didn't you come to Rocco's wedding?"

Distress marred her gaze, before she composed herself enough to hide it. Her green eyes were huge in her oval face, the pallor of her skin parchment white. "I've been busy with work. Not all of us have turned our dreams into such an amazing reality as you have done with your global real estate company."

"I started with nothing more than you did, Clio. I never took a penny from my parents after they disowned me."

"Christian told me. After Serena, you—" She must have caught the blaze of anger in his gaze because she grimaced and continued, "After everything that happened in the last semester, you never looked back once.

"So stop blaming me alone for a friendship that didn't last. In the first couple of years, Christian kept me abreast of what was happening with you guys. After that, it was hard to miss your success with all four of you hitting young millionaires' lists left and right. But I'm not bitter enough to bemoan your success, Stefan."

"I'm asking now, *bella*. What happened to your dreams, Clio?"

"Reality happened, okay? I discovered how hard it is to actually make it in this world. So kudos to you for doing it." She took another calming breath. "Tell me about Rocco's wedding." It was obvious that she wanted to turn the conversation away from her life, but still, warmth spilled into her green eyes as she said Rocco's name. "It would have been something to see Rocco dance to the tunes of the woman he fell so hard for. Olivia Fitzgerald must be really special."

The wistfulness in her gaze before she looked around herself and covered it up tugged at his curiosity. "Olivia is definitely something, and Rocco is well and truly caught."

He noted the way her gaze kept going to the entrance to the terrace, the same revolving door that Jackson and the blonde had walked through. "It was only a plane ride away, Clio. If it's money for the plane ticket, you could have just asked one of us."

"I'm not destitute, Stefan," she said tiredly, as if she would do anything if he just left her alone. "After Christian paid my rent for a few months that one time, I managed fine."

Shock reverberated through Stefan.

Christian had helped Clio once with the rent? Had it been that bad for her?

But he had no doubt as to why Christian wouldn't have breathed a word. His friend had grown up in poverty on the streets of Athens, was the one who really understood what it meant to make ends meet when you started with nothing.

He understood why it would have been Christian that Clio had gone to. But still, he didn't like that things had been so bad for her and he hadn't even had an inkling of it.

He stared at her anew.

There was no emotion, not even bitterness, in her tone. Only an underlying urgency and fear prompted by what, he had no idea.

It had to be something related to Jackson.

A renewed purpose filled him. He had to help her get out of whatever it was.

"If you ever needed something, you only had to ask."

"I don't want charity. Yours or anyone else's. I paid Christian back when I was able to. I'm fine now."

"Then why did you not come to the wedding? Why did you blanch when you saw me?"

"I told you. I've had too many things going on and—"

"Is it that or is the fact that your new associations and your new way of life don't let you see your old friends anymore?"

She paled. "Whatever it is that you're implying, say it straight to my face, Stefan. It's not like you to worry about someone else's feelings, is it?"

"Jackson Smith."

A stillness came over her and Stefan knew. Whatever it was that robbed all color from her skin, that made a shadow of Clio, it was Jackson. "What…what do you mean?" He saw her throat swallow forcibly.

"Are you not well, *bella*?"

She jerked away from him, her breath coming in sharp bursts. "What. About. Jackson, Stefan?"

"Jackson is a crook. A polished, smooth-talking, self-centered crook. The best thing I can say about him is that he doesn't lack for female company wherever he goes."

Her brittle laughter interrupted him. "I could say the

same or even less about you. A Slavic model and the ripples that she created just a couple of months ago come to mind." A feverish gleam entered her eyes. "What was it? 'Bianco's last name should really be Bastard,'" she finished with a mutinous gleam. "You have been dubbed the One-Date Wonder because you won't even the see the same woman twice."

Her defense of that crook infuriated Stefan. "You have no idea what Jackson could be up to. His business practices are extremely murky. I have been looking for proof for a long time to pin him for it. He's a greedy bastard, a leech who will use anyone to climb the ladder a little more, will use any means, even illegal ones to get what he wants. In straight words, he's scum through and through. Whatever connection you have with him, cut it and walk away, before he brings you down with him."

Every ounce of color fled from her face, leaving a pale, tight mask behind. "I don't believe you. I know that Jackson can be brash and even uncouth sometimes, but he…"

"Then you've also become a fool and are not worth my time or advice."

Fury that she would put him on the same level as Jackson left a bad taste in his mouth. This was not the woman he had known and admired once.

"Or maybe this is the life you lead now, Clio. Maybe walking away from wealth and the status you were born to didn't work out quite like you thought it would. Maybe the facade of status and wealth that Jackson provides you makes being part of his crooked schemes worth it."

Something flittered in her gaze, and against every instinct that warned him to walk away, Stefan stayed. Instead of the anger he expected, hurt wreathed her features. And again, this pale imitation of the old Clio he had known once twisted a knot in his gut.

"You don't think that really."

"A decade is a long time. You might be just as power hungry and itching to be kept like most women I know."

"And you must have really become a cold bastard to be able to say that to me."

Her words fell away like water on rocks. Had he become sentimental about her because he had known her a decade ago?

Clio was no different.

Women with self-respect, women who weren't out for everything they could get could be counted on one hand. Like Rocco's Olivia.

"Touché, *bella*. Maybe we are strangers to each other."

"With nothing more to say to each other."

She looked as if she was caught in a trap with no way out. It would haunt him if he walked away now.

"*Dio*, Clio…are you in some kind of trouble? Just tell me how you know him."

Her chin lifted. As if she was bracing herself for attack.

"I work for him, have done for five years now. He gave me a job when no one would hire me, Stefan, showed me a way to make it in New York when I would have returned home to England with shame on my face. I have to believe that you're mistaken. I have to believe for my own sake that everything you're saying…" As erect and stiff as her shoulders were, she trembled. "Jackson's my fiancé."

"You are…" Gritting his jaw, Stefan curtailed the stinging response that rose to his lips, waited for the shock that was reverberating inside him to abate.

The fact that she had mentioned her engagement to Jackson as a second thought, that she had almost swayed while saying it—nothing could dilute the acidic taste that filled him.

How could Clio, of all the women in the world, be engaged to marry Jackson Smith? Had she changed that much?

Was it all shine and no substance to Clio either?

A memory from a long time ago of a laughing Clio, her lustrous red hair flying behind her, cycling across the campus from one class to the next, challenging him to a race, slammed into him.

Against the backdrop of a lot of ugly memories of New York that persisted in his mind, he could do nothing but let himself be washed in the wake of this one.

"'Two roads diverged in a wood, and I—I took the road less traveled by, and that has made all the difference,'" he said, quoting her favorite line by Frost.

A gasp fell from her mouth, the sheen of tears turning her eyes into glittering emeralds. "I used to think of you as a firestorm, Clio. Vibrant, fierce and so unafraid." His pulse quickened as the scent of her skin teased him. "I used to think you were the strongest woman I had ever met.

"Don't tell me everything is okay in your life, *bella*. Because I can see it's not." He placed his hand on one bony shoulder and squeezed. Felt the tremble that racked her.

She looked up at him, shock and disbelief written all over her face.

"I'll be at the Chatsfield for a couple of days. If you need something, *anything*, come see me.

"We can have a drink and I'll tell you about this girl I met on the first day of university, looking for art class. Her hair the color of molten fire, her smile as big as the ocean…the very joy in every step she took that she was finally free…

"She was a sight to behold.

"Two years later, she bet the champion rowing team of four—" he was smiling now, thinking of himself, Zayed, Rocco and Christian brimming with cocky confidence, amazed at the redhead who dared challenge them while every other woman worshipped the ground they walked on "—that she would walk naked across the university lawn rather than cheer them in the final tournament. Told them their arrogant heads were already full of themselves.

"And the night they did win that match, she ran through the lawn, fully dressed and completely sloshed, like a streak of lightning. Because she thought they would demand that she pay.

"I don't think I remember ever laughing so much as I did that night."

With a hand that was not quite steady, he wiped the one tear that rolled down her cheek. Whispered the motto by which he and the rest of the Columbia Four lived by. Words that had served Rocco, Christian, Zayed and him well, more than once.

"Memento vivere, bella."

CHAPTER TWO

REMEMBER TO LIVE...

Clio leaned against the balcony, her legs trembling beneath her, her heart thumping wildly against her rib cage.

A motto that Rocco, Christian, Zayed and Stefan lived by... She had always laughed at the way they quoted it, at how they used it to conquer the world that had been their playground...

Laughed it away so easily because, of course, she had been a shining example of it...

Had she been that girl once?

Stefan's words swept through her with the force of a tsunami, holding up a picture of the woman she had been so long ago that it was almost like a figment of her imagination.

That Clio had been full of fire and dreams for the future, determined to take on life on her terms.

And yet, here she was today, waiting for the man who had professed to love her. Letting him rule her choice of clothing, her time and even what she did with her life. Waiting for him to look at her again as he had done three years ago. Wishing desperately that he still loved her.

Letting her life pass by with a sigh, her opinions and her words swallowed and locked in her throat.

How had she become this person? Where the hell was Jackson?

Sick of waiting another moment longer, she made her

way into the corridor. The empty space sent her heart thudding in her chest as she took the staircase to the lower floor.

And stilled as a smoky, drawling laugh and the accompanying husky female whisper reached her.

A dreadful suspicion gathered momentum and rushed toward her like a freight train. Every step felt like one toward her own doom. Her skin crawled as a sensual gasp filled the air, and the whispers of clothes and limbs punctured the silence.

"Jackson…oh, baby…I can't do this anymore, Jackson. I love you and I… Tell her it's over, Jackson."

Tears filled Clio's eyes as she stood there, her breath suspended in her throat, her world falling apart around her. Her hands turned into fists by her side, and she shoved one in her mouth to stop the shocked gasp from making itself heard.

She heard more grunts and a soft curse fall from Jackson and instantly, her mind supplied the image required. "Just a few more months, baby. You know how much we need her connections.

"Clio is blue-blooded aristocracy, the likes of whom I won't meet again. Did you see the sheer size and scope of Jane Alcott's estates? A few more clients like that, and we will be set."

"But, Jackson…" Clio could just imagine the pout of Ashley's voluptuous mouth, "I'll be showing by then. Is this how you want our new life to begin? Me hiding in case Ms. Stiff and Proper sees me while you pretend to be her loving fiancé? The thought of you touching her makes me so…"

Ashley is pregnant… It seemed there was no end to the knocks coming her way…

Jackson spoke amidst rattling breaths. "I have no desire to touch her. And you very well know that I have no strength left after one of our afternoon appointments to do so even if I were inclined."

Clio slapped her hands over her ears as she heard Ashley's satisfied laugh.

"Just give me a couple more months." Saccharine warmth dripped from Jackson's voice. "She's still very useful to us. Once I have used up all the connections Clio can provide for us, I'll get rid of her. Until then, appearances are crucial."

"If she backs out before then?"

"Backs out of what? For all her claims of walking away from her family and the man they wanted her to marry, Clio's desperate to be loved, desperate to feel that she's succeeded at something even if it's just scoring a man." There was no hesitation in Jackson's voice. Only the absolute truth as he believed it to be. "The woman she is now, there's no other man who would touch Clio Norwood with a pole, much less want her."

Bile crawled up Clio's throat and she turned away from the door. Pushing the heavy door to the staircase, she only got up one group of stairs before her legs gave out and she collapsed onto the grimy floor.

Desperate to be loved, desperate to feel that she's succeeded at something...

Beating back her head against the wall, Clio closed her eyes, shutting off the tears that threatened to deluge her. Still, a few drops leaked through her tightly shut lids.

How could she have misjudged Jackson so badly? How could she have not seen this coming? How many times did she need to learn this lesson? She had never been valued for anything more than her father's name, had never been valued for herself.

However far she ran, her name and everything it entailed caught up with her. Fury and self-disgust unlike she had ever known slammed into her gut.

For months, she had let Jackson walk over her, she had let Ashley make a mockery of her in front of friends.

There had been too many business dinners to attend,

too many charity galas they needed to be seen at—dressed in designer clothes and sipping champagne, instead of where she preferred to be—behind the scenes getting her hands dirty.

There had been too much of displaying themselves rather than doing anything of substance. Too much of putting herself on parade on Jackson's arm, too much of talking about her parents and her family's aristocratic background and connections.

Too much of being stifled by rules, weighed down by expectations. Too much of being a Norwood, daughter of one of the most powerful aristocratic families in Britain, too much of being the Manhattan elite, power-hungry financier Jackson Smith's fiancée.

Too little of being herself, of just being Clio.

All her life, she had craved her father's approval, even when she hadn't fit right with her family's aristocratic connections. She'd stupidly hoped he would be proud of her if she did as he asked of her.

Had tried to make herself the perfect daughter. Until she found out he had arranged her marriage and choked at the very ropes she had bound around herself.

And she had fallen into the same trap with Jackson.

All the signs had been there and she had been too blind to see them, too desperate to need something in her life to be a success.

She had led herself to the very same place she had left in her home country over a decade ago, into the same life where she couldn't breathe.

Every uncomfortable feeling she had repressed, every doubt she had swallowed so that she didn't mess up another one of his meetings and parties, suddenly balled up in her throat, choking her breath.

Her identity had somehow fractured and attached itself in pieces to Jackson's.

And all for what?

So that he could cheat on her, so that he could impregnate his assistant.

Her love, her fears, hadn't mattered to Jackson at all. And not seeing that truth had all been her fault.

CHAPTER THREE

"I'M SORRY, MA'AM. I can't allow you to go up to Mr. Bianco's suite."

Clio heard the receptionist behind the huge swathe of pristine black marble and looked around herself in confusion. Had she inquired about Stefan? Where had she walked to?

Turning around, she swept her gaze over the quiet and ultraluxurious lounge at the Chatsfield New York. A bank of glass-walled elevators stood to the side.

Utter silence reigned over the marble-floored lounge, the humdrum of quiet efficiency amidst the flowing humanity of Manhattan outside creating a sharp contrast.

The lavish interior of the famous hotel filtered in through her slowly.

"Do you want me to let him know of your arrival, Ms....?"

Blinking, Clio pulled her attention back to the young man. "Clio. Just Clio," she said, working her mouth to make the sound. Just the thought of saying Norwood sent a chill through her. Her entire body felt as if it was operating on some kind of auto mechanism she hadn't known she possessed.

Why else would she come to a man whose power and ambition were ten times those of Jackson? A man who had looked at her as if she had somehow tainted herself just by her association with Jackson?

"Wait, Miss...Ms....Clio, hold on."

Coloring at the curious perusal of the receptionist, Clio wrapped her arms around herself. "I'm sorry for troubling you. I have to leave."

She hadn't even realized how or when she had decided to walk to the Chatsfield, to see Stefan. The enigmatic green gaze and scornful mouth rose in front of her and she shook herself. No, she had no strength to expose herself to his brand of truth and evaluation, didn't have the strength to fare against the memory of a woman she didn't even remember being once.

His disappointment earlier still stung like a slap.

If she went to him the way she was feeling right now, he would lacerate her with his ruthless words, would peel away any remnants of self-respect she still had left.

The thought of telling him what she had heard, the thought of his reaction got her to move as nothing else could.

She took a few steps toward the revolving glass doors when she heard her name called again.

"Ms. Clio, Mr. Bianco authorized a permanent key card for you with us. At all our international branches. He left very specific instructions that we were to provide anything you asked for, anything you needed, should you come."

The receptionist placed the key card on the gleaming counter and pulled his hand back.

As if he knew how close to breaking point she was. As if she were a wild animal he needed to treat with the utmost care. Something in his kind gaze, something in the cajoling tone of his voice shook Clio out of the fog she was functioning in.

Was this what she had become? A woman so lost in life that she had reduced a perfect stranger to pitying her?

She didn't know what she wanted to do, she didn't know how to take the next step in her life. She felt utterly lost, alone.

The fact that all she wanted to do was crawl into the

nearest hole and never emerge scraped her raw. And yet, something in her, some small part of her that refused to whimper like a victim, had brought her here.

Her career, her life, her self-respect and her heart—everything lay in ragged tatters around her feet.

She knew that she needed help. To figure out how to do the one thing that burned inside her while everything else lay in ashes.

She grabbed the key card and palmed the smooth surface. Forced herself to put one foot in front of the other, to take a deep, purging breath. The quiet swish of the lift as it bore her to the fifty-second floor pinged against her tautly stretched nerves.

When the doors finally opened, she stepped out onto an enormous foyer boasting four balconies with glass railings that provided breathtaking views of the one of the world's finest cities.

It was like a castle built amidst the clouds.

Walking past a gold-embossed statue in the middle of the foyer, she reached the lounge. A champagne-and-brown color scheme reigned, with glittering burnished-gold and deep red accessories here and there that matched the white-hot temperament of the man she had once known.

Although the Stefan she had met this evening had been coldly ruthless.

What the hell was she even doing here?

Just as she turned in the direction of the elevator, his silky smooth question rang out.

"You're leaving already?"

Clutching her eyes closed, Clio willed herself to calm down. In a helpless way that made her totally nauseous, she was glad that he had spotted her before she had made a hasty exit.

Because now, she knew Stefan wouldn't let her leave. Now, if she could just find the strength to say what she had come to say without betraying herself…

Every doubt she was harboring ground to a halt as he moved into the lounge with a lithe grace that she followed as if she was mesmerized.

A plush white towel wrapped around his narrow hips contrasted sharply against a tanned chest. Droplets of water clung to chest hair that covered ropes of well-defined muscles. His freshly shaved jawline glinted with that trademark arrogance of his while his olive green gaze pinned her to the spot.

Awareness sliced through Clio like a physical shove to her senses and she swayed where she stood. It was like a deluge of flood over drought-ridden land.

"Clio, is everything all right?" he said, tossing a white towel over his nape that fell onto his chest.

Clio came back to the earth with a thump. Suddenly, asking Stefan for help felt like the most absurd idea she had ever thought of.

Before she could blink, he covered the distance between them. The scent of him, raw and masculine, was like a whiplash that slammed her breath in her throat.

Shaking her head, she pushed her hair back. "I'm fine. Can I have something to drink?"

For a few seconds, he stood there staring at her.

Tall, impossibly wide, six feet three inches of prime Sicilian male, and all his focus was on her. His eyes perused her with a leisurely intensity that made her feel exposed, raw.

Not that she trusted her body's response.

Finally, he moved to the glittering bar that covered one side of the lounge. "What would you like to drink?"

"Just some water, please." There was a false comfort in talking about something so mundane. Maybe because it reminded her that the world did not fall away even through the earthquake in her life. "Alcohol gives me—"

"A migraine, I know. Are they still as bad as they used to be?"

He had remembered. Clio squashed the spurt of warmth

that bloomed in her chest with ruthless will. So one of the youngest millionaires in the world had a good memory. Not a big surprise. "I never found anything to help me. So I don't touch it," she said, shrugging.

The sound of the refrigerator opening, the soft clink of the ice cubes against the glass punctured the silence that swathed them with awkwardness.

She hadn't even told him why she was here. And he hadn't asked.

Yet, it felt as if there was something in the air, an imbalance of power, a swirl of currents eddying around them, caging them together in the cavernous lounge. And she recoiled at adding to it by telling him what had happened tonight.

Would he laugh at her stupidity that she hadn't even seen through Jackson's facade for so long?

She grabbed the glass from him, and took a greedy gulp. All the while, he stood there like a dark specter, watching her, assessing her. And somehow she had a feeling, he found her wanting.

She had fallen in her own eyes. *Did it matter if she did in his?* a rebellious part of her mocked.

The answer had to be no because she didn't have a single feeling to spare for him. There was nothing but cold will to keep her going.

"I'm sorry about intruding on you unannounced," she said, once the cold water brought feeling back into her throat. "I didn't even realize I had started walking toward…"

Catching the gleam of mockery in his green gaze, she faltered.

He took the glass from her shaking fingers. "Clio Norwood—epitome of good manners and decorum, even as she's falling apart."

"I'm not falling apart."

His blunt-tipped fingers landed on her jaw and tilted her face up.

Panic chasing her stringent awareness of him, she caught

his wrist to push it away. The pressure of his fingers increased.

"Then why are you so jumpy?"

There was no sympathy in his voice and for that she was a thousand times grateful. One kind word from him would break the small thread that was holding her together.

Falling apart, in front of him, was not a choice.

"I'm not. I just…" A ball of tears tightened her throat.

"Tell me what's going on, Clio."

The inherent command in his tone somehow grounded her.

Instead of jerking away from his touch, she slowly pushed it back. But the rasp of his hair-roughened wrist, the strong tendons of it, was too much sensation. She dropped his hand, her pulse thudding too loud.

"Have you eaten dinner?"

"No."

"How did you get here?"

She raised her gaze. "What?"

"To the Chatsfield?"

"I walked."

"From where?"

"From the dinner party."

"At the Empire State Building?"

"Yes."

He cursed so vehemently that Clio hugged herself instinctively. "That's almost fifteen blocks from here and it's nine-thirty at night. What the hell is wrong with you that you would walk at night in New York of all places?"

She remained mute, no response rising in the face of his valid point.

He sighed. "Finish that water and then order something from room service. I'll get dressed and be back. And then you can tell me why you look like you—"

Anxiety hit her in waves. If he disappeared, she knew she would lose whatever it was that had brought her this far.

Saving face in front of him would become more important than moving on in her life.

"No, wait. Don't leave. I…"

"Then get rid of that look in your eyes, *bella*," he said. "I can't stand it." A hint of emotion colored that bland statement.

"What look?"

Pushing his tensile body into her space, he folded his hands. The muscles in his biceps curled enticingly and Clio choked back hysteria. Her life was falling apart, and yet it seemed the sight of Stefan half-naked could distract her as nothing else could.

"Like you're terrified of me," he said through gritted teeth. "We might have become strangers to each other but I would never hurt you, *bella*. Whatever Jackson did, you need to shake yourself out of it." His voice fell as if she were a wounded animal he was persuading into his care.

"I'm not a danger to you, Clio."

Oh, but he was, Clio admitted, her pulse skyrocketing.

If Jackson had reduced her to a shadow of herself over the years, Stefan could destroy the small part of her that was still intact. That he knew what she had been once and what she was now, it was a weapon he could wield with ease and without emotion, if he didn't like what she was about to say.

The young man she had known at Columbia had not only been idealistic but also kind, with a rosy view of the world.

This man he was now, he rattled Clio on so many levels.

But she had no intention of ever letting a man define her sense of self. Ever again.

The thought gave her the courage to say what she wanted to. "I decided to take you up on your offer. I need your…I need help, Stefan."

Something infinitesimal flashed in his brooding gaze, gone before she could read it. His defined jaw hardened. He moved to a small side table with delicately carved legs, and pulled out a checkbook.

He flipped it open with a pen poised in his left hand. That familiar sight of him balancing the book on his right forearm brought forth such a strong memory that she almost didn't hear him when he said, "How much do you need?"

Her jaw falling open, Clio stared at him. Acid crawled up her throat and she forced herself to hold his gaze, realizing what his look had meant.

He thought she had come to him for money.

Even as he had reminded her of what she had been, it was clear that Stefan had already written her off as a lost cause.

It rankled just as much as Jackson's treacherous perfidy did; it tore her in half that she had brought this on herself. But it was high time she started fighting for herself, too. High time she started growing a backbone.

"How much, Clio?"

"Will you give me as much as I want, Stefan? How about a million dollars?" Something in her challenged him, pushed to see how far he would go.

He didn't even blink. "A million it will be, *bella*. I will tell my finance guy that this year our charity contribution is going to the Clio Norwood Foundation."

I don't want your charity.

Swallowing back the bile his offhand comment provoked, she reminded herself to not flinch, to not betray the hurt that lanced through her.

She had no idea why she was inflicting this on herself, but she couldn't stop.

"And if I come back for more?"

"I'll give you more." He threw the checkbook on the coffee table between them, the gesture so full of powerful arrogance and a masculine elegance that Clio forgot what had prompted it. Even half-naked as he was, power and ruthlessness emanated from every cell in him.

"You can have as much as you want, Clio. All you would have to do is walk away from that crook. No matter how deep you are in, you can walk away."

"Why? Why would you help me?"

"Once, you were my friend. Once, I used to think the world of you. Seeing you like this…"

Some unnamed emotion flickered in his eyes and Clio stared anew. His face transformed so much when a hint of emotion touched it that it was like seeing a shadow of the old Stefan.

"If I can help you get away from—" he scowled as if he hated even saying Jackson's name again "—I'll save you, even if it has to be from yourself. It's like taking a friend or a family member to a rehabilitation clinic for treatment for addiction."

"Even though you think I'm not worth the ground I'm standing on?"

His dark smile didn't falter for a second. "Your words, *bella*, not mine." A blast of cold solidified in her core and Clio shivered.

It was one thing to think that of herself, another to hear someone confirm it. But with Stefan, there was nothing but honesty. Cutting, lacerating honesty, but honesty all the same.

His gaze swept over her, lingering and intense. "But, yes, even then. I would do the same for Rocco, Christian and Zayed, too."

The Columbia Four's friendship, the inviolate bond they had forged with each other, she had always been envious of it. To be included now as something he had to salvage from the wreck she'd made of herself… "Wow, at least in one regard, I'm in illustrious company, aren't I?"

He moved around the coffee table, and it was like watching a wild animal move. With grace and purpose.

The moment he was within touching distance, everything within Clio retreated inward into a tight ball. But still, the heat of his body incited a trembling in her very bones.

The breadth of his frame swathed her as he bent down.

"Do not ask a question of me if you don't have the constitution for truth, Clio."

Her brain taken over with issuing flight responses, Clio nodded dumbly.

Stefan Bianco was a Sicilian alpha male in his prime.

Physically magnificent, powerful beyond her wildest imagination, ruthlessly rich. A potent combination of masculinity and heat that could probably compel a stone to react if he so intended.

A woman like her, with her very sense of self battered and beaten down, was nothing. She wrapped her hands around herself, as if it could corral his presence and her reaction.

If she wasn't careful, he would overpower her so much that she would get swept away in unraveling that enigmatic disinterest he projected so easily. As so many women did—deluding themselves that they could melt the icy heart beneath the fiery exterior of his Sicilian temperament.

Stefan had buried his heart so deep and so long ago that he didn't even have one anymore, she sensed. Stepping away from him, she shook herself free of his magnetic pull. Met his gaze head-on. "I never want to hear anything but the truth from you, Stefan."

"Deal," he said with an indulgent smile that was more like a threat than a reassuring promise. "Now it's time to put your cards on the table, *bella*. Without fear."

She knew exactly where she stood with him; she would always know.

His brand of friendship—eviscerating and without an ounce of pretension—was what she needed to remake herself, to redefine herself. Stefan was the perfect path for her to walk on toward becoming her own woman again.

"As gratifying as it is to learn I could have millions if I just made myself your charity case, I didn't come here for money. I want nothing from you for free."

"What do you want, then?"

Her chest felt so tight that she had to break his gaze. Had to force herself to speak past the sound of Jackson's and Ashley's combined laughter resonating through her.

Jackson's cheating on her, using her for her connections, reducing her entire identity to the value she provided him in his blasted business, scraped her raw. But that he could be so casually cruel about her feelings, that he would betray every aspect of their lives together, that he would laugh at her fears and insecurities behind her back…it festered inside her like a putrefied wound.

It tainted every aspect of her so much that she was beginning to despise herself.

And she wouldn't be able to move forward, wouldn't be able to look herself in the eye unless she showed him that he couldn't do this to her without realizing the consequences. Unless she proved to him and herself that she was more than what he had called her.

"I want to teach Jackson a lesson he will never forget."

Cold—blanching and eviscerating—dawned in Stefan's gaze and he stepped away as if she was the very plague. His jaw clenched so tight that it was a wonder he spoke through it. "I will not play petty games so that you can make him jealous and win him back. If that's why you came, get out. *Now.* Before I physically restrain you from going back to that leech."

"I don't want to make him jealous. I want to remove Jackson from every part of my life. I don't want even his shadow to touch me anymore."

"That is as simple as walking away, Clio."

"Not without making him realize what he's done to me."

Disbelief shone in his eyes. "Earlier, you wouldn't believe a word I said. How do I know you won't go running back to him the minute he starts whispering words of love again?"

"Earlier, I was a fool who'd have done anything for the man I loved. Now…I feel nothing but disgust and pity for that woman. My skin crawls when I think that I stayed all these years... Does that satisfy you? Or do you want me to prostrate myself before you're ready to believe me?"

His gaze encompassed her from top to toe as though he was enjoying the idea of her prostrating herself. By sheer will, she stood still under that assessing gaze.

"You're angry and emotional right now. Tomorrow, you'll forgive him and crawl back to him—"

"Listen to my proposal first. Then make your decision."

She was so tired of men playing their games with her, controlling her, defining her, owning her joys and her sorrows.

First her father and then Jackson...

So tired of losing herself, again and again. The irony of appealing to another man for help, of letting him see her darkest fears, a man who was a hundred times more powerful and ruthless than Jackson or her father, wasn't lost on her.

But Jackson had been wrong. She still had one avenue left and she was going to throw herself into it.

"Do you want to expose Jackson's reality to the world?"

Something shifted in his expression, a watchful uncoiling of his rigid stance. He was hooked. For the first time in months, Clio felt a surge of positivity fill her.

"Throwing a million dollars at you is easy. What you're suggesting is far more elaborate and requires a great deal of my actual involvement."

"But you'll do it," she said, forcing confidence into her tone.

Heat flared in his gaze at the vehemence of her statement. She braced herself, expecting him to cut her down.

"Why?"

"Because I saw it in your face tonight just as you saw whatever you did in mine.

"When I said he was my fiancé, there was such anger, such distaste in your gaze. I don't know how or what he did to you, but I know that you won't forgive and forget."

His gaze swept over her face with a thoroughly cold appraisal. "I see that there's still a bit of the old Clio in you, *bella*."

"You have found the weak link in Jackson's life. It's me." Her voice wobbled on the last bit, the very venom that Jackson's words caused in her coating her throat.

"I will bring that man down if we start on this path. There will be no half measures, no backing out. No going back to him. Ever."

"I'm not weak, Stefan, not in this. I swallowed the disgust that was roiling through me today, and came to you without his knowledge."

"Tell me what happened."

For a second, Clio could only stare at the authority with which he demanded an answer.

"Does it matter what happened? If I have to face myself in the mirror, if I have to…I'll bring you anything you need about Jackson's business and his hedge fund company. But only if you agree to my proposal."

"What is your proposal, Clio?"

Clio stared at Stefan and willed the words to come, willed herself to put the last part of her plan into words. It had been gathering in the back of her mind like a tsunami, shaking everything in its path, laughing at her weak will, her fears.

She couldn't back out now, as scary as it was to tie her fate to this man even temporarily.

Stefan Bianco, once a cherished friend and now a ruthless stranger, would be the fire through which she would have to walk. And once she emerged from that fire, no man would ever have the power to hurt her again.

No man would even come close.

"I want you to profess undying love to me. In a gesture that captures media attention. I want you to get engaged to me, turn all that brooding arrogance into possessive, fiery love for me. I want you to lend me the might of your status

ff, cherishing that friendship more; then he had met and
llen in love with Serena.

His mind was more than eager to wander on the paths
ey had never gone on, that they could take now.

But there were plenty of uncomplicated, desirable women
the world for his taste. Ones who didn't look as if they
ere barely holding on.

Clio, for him, clearly needed to be in the Do Not Touch
mp.

He couldn't help teasing her, though. "As far as I can see,
u're in good shape, so that's good."

Utter silence stretched between them, the moment build-
g and building.

"Since we're counting if I'll be useful to you or not, are
u considering my proposal?"

There was a self-deprecation in her tone that masked
mething beneath. The way she held herself so stiff, the
y her fingers clutched her opposite hands—Stefan knew
was fear.

Realizing how close she was to falling apart only made
n wonder at the strength of her. But whatever Jackson had
ne, she was still riding that wave of adrenaline.

Which meant she would crash soon.

And he had no doubt that she would back away, even re-
l at the very idea of them joining forces to bring down
kson.

The young woman he had known at Columbia had posed the biggest heart he had ever seen, had possessed
zing capacity for love and forgiveness.

hat she had come to him like this, that Clio was con-
ing this path, spoke of the damage Jackson must have
to her.

ry filled Stefan that Jackson's ambition had led to this.
didn't take care of her, she could end up like Marco.
rse.

as the ruthless playboy who wouldn't look twice at the same
woman much less have a relationship with her.

"And I want all this done in a way that Jackson can't
turn his head, can't even blink without our engagement
splashed in his face.

"Then, I'll bring you everything you need to expose him."

CHAPTER FOUR

"No."

The word fell from his mouth and boomeranged in the cavernous lounge even before Stefan processed Clio's outrageous proposition. The very thought of tying himself to a woman, any woman, filled his veins with ice.

And to someone like Clio, whom he had liked once…it was unbearable even in thought.

Rubbing his hand over his jaw, he looked up at her.

Desperation and something else danced beneath the steady look she cast him. Her fingers as she settled them over her forearms left pink marks revealing how tightly she was holding on.

Her hair was beginning to fall away from the tight knot at the back of her head. Still dressed in the black sleeveless dress that somehow leached all the color from her face, he knew she had come to him directly from the party.

Had somehow found the strength to come to him.

He shoved away the protectiveness that rose like a storm within him, to be discerned later.

It had been a while since a woman had surprised him with her words or actions.

The fact that it was Clio, a woman he had written off as a lost cause, intensified the surprise.

"As tempting as your proposal is, I have no intention of associating myself with a woman romantically, *bella*. Even for a pretense. Even for a few months. Even for saving a friend. I will never be good to the woman who [ ] that role in my life, Clio."

Her chin tilted down, but there was determin[ ] her gaze. "It's just a pretense, Stefan. I won't ask [ ] of you."

"No."

"Then you get nothing from me about Jackso[ ] gaze flashed with determination. "And just so yo[ ] what you're saying no to, I'm a board member on h[ ] pany.

"Of course, I have been nothing but a figureh[ ] these years but at least it's unrestricted access. To h[ ] pany's finances, his bank accounts, even his offsh[ ] vestments."

"Anything shady ever caught your interest?"

She shook her head. "I've never had reason to d[ ] him."

"The minute the media links my name with you[ ] a whisper, Jackson will shut you out. You'll be of n[ ] me. Our antipathy is mutual."

Exhaling slowly, she loosened her fingers, her [ ] pable in the way her features relaxed. "Obvious[ ] first time plotting something vicious like this, so [ ] to excuse me if I don't go all *Kill Bill* on you righ[ ] fan. I'm thinking on my feet here."

He laughed, glad to see a spot of color in [ ] again. "Then let's put shopping for a yellow sui[ ] rai sword on the agenda, *si*? First stop will b[ ]

An almost smile glimmered around her p[ ] Stefan had the oddest urge to tease it out o[ ] way flashes of the old Clio peeked through [ ] and defeat in her eyes stirred him.

A challenge—that's what she could b[ ] he let her. Because, even a decade ago, h[ ] had pursued her doggedly that first year[ ]

But once they had become true frien[ ]

And the thought of anything happening to her at the hands of Jackson drove him wild with panic.

With a control that had taken him years to hone, he forced himself to sound casual. "Your proposal is beneficial to me. So yes, I'm considering it."

"What do I have to do to convince you completely?" she retorted instantly and he found relief in her mutinous gaze.

What he needed now was time with Clio.

Time in which Clio didn't see Jackson and revert back to that pale shadow she had been earlier tonight. Time in which she would crash from whatever was driving her right this minute and consider going back to him again.

Time in which he could keep her close. And even if things didn't work out as per the plan between them, he had no intention of letting her go back to that man.

Even as he had struggled with getting a handle on his intense reaction to seeing her again, he had come to terms with some of it.

He felt responsible for Clio. It didn't matter where it grew from, only that he did.

"I will accept your deal based on one condition."

Clio forced herself to shrug, to affect a casualness that she was far from feeling. She had known the man he was today wouldn't just follow along with her plans.

That he would demand something from her struck fear in her, though. "I have nothing else to give you. My career, my life, even my savings account is tied to Jackson and his company. As of this moment, I don't even have a place to go back to."

"That works out perfectly for what I have in mind, then."

"Was that my miserable life that you were referring to just now?"

A dark smile turned the corners of his serious mouth upward. "If you want to be publicly engaged to me, if you want me to act the part of besotted fiancé, first you have to prove it to me that you have enough guts to see through this whole thing. I won't let you go back on it when it's time for your part."

"I already told you that this is…"

He shook his head. "My way or no way, Clio."

She blew out a long breath, her aristocratic nose flaring with her struggle for control. "Fine. What do I have to do to prove that I'll see this through, that you won't have a hysterical female who's dying to go back to Jackson?"

"You have to come with me to Christian and Alessandra's wedding," he said.

It was the last thing she expected him to say. The last thing she wanted to do in the world.

Coming to see Stefan tonight, she was still amazed at her own strength in managing it. But seeing Rocco, Christian and Zayed, seeing the disbelief and pity that would fill their faces when they saw her, she didn't have the heart for it.

"There's nothing you will gain by dragging me to Christian's wedding."

"That's for me to decide," he said, arrogant implacability in his tone.

"Stefan, listen to me. I'll go back to Jackson tonight and pretend like nothing happened. Even as nauseous as it makes me to do it. For the next week, I'll continue to keep my mouth shut like I did over the last few years and let him think I'm still the same, spineless Clio." Just thinking of it made her skin crawl. "I'll wait until you return from Christian's wedding. That's innumerable chances for me to back out of this thing, by your logic. But I'll be here, waiting. Then you'll know that I'm serious."

"No."

"Why the hell do you care if I go to Christian's wedding or not?"

"If you want to start a new life, *bella*, why not start it with coming back to your old friends?"

"I can't, Stefan. I don't have the…"

"What?"

He reached out to her and pulled her hand into his. Immediately, her fingers stiffened in his but he didn't let go. "Neither of us is going to benefit by lying to each other or by treading carefully, Clio. If this pretense has any chance to work, it has to be anything but between us. *Capisce, bella?*"

"Yes, but I don't see the point in carrying the pretense forward to our friends, too. Will you lie to Rocco, Christian and Zayed, Stefan? Will you be able to?"

"If we want the world to buy into our shock engagement, yes. Leave them to me. You…you will not breathe a word to another soul what's happening between us.

"With Rocco already married and Christian doing the same, the whole world's eyes are already on the Columbia Four. Won't be difficult to get them to buy that I'm following in my friends' footsteps and looking forward to a happily-ever-after with the woman I adore."

"I won't be able to pull it off. Deception and lying have never come easy to me."

"Don't worry, Clio. You'll be just as good or even better at pulling this off as any other woman I've ever known."

"Stop insulting me, Stefan. I'm not one of your—"

"The jury's still out on that one," he cut her off without blinking an eye, without an ounce of emotion. "Think of it this way, *bella*. For us to begin a pretend engagement that the media and the whole world will eat up, we need to lay the groundwork.

"And what better way to start a lifelong love affair that will be the talk of the world than going to an old, mutual friend's wedding? Every way I look at it, this is what we need to start our fairy-tale romance."

A fairy-tale romance with one of the most gorgeous, arrogant, hard-hearted men she had ever met…it was a fate that would have sent Clio running a decade ago.

It had been the fate she had walked away from.

But joining forces with Stefan in this was her choice, she reminded herself.

Meeting his gaze, she nodded. "Fine. Let's go to Christian's wedding. But I have to see Jackson tomorrow."

"No."

"If I have to look through his finances, I can't walk away from him yet."

"Then I will come with you."

"No. I won't fall apart, Stefan. Not tomorrow, not in the coming days."

"Where the hell have you been, Clio? You don't answer your cell, you're not at work…"

Her breath balling in her throat, Clio stilled as she walked into the lounge of the flat she had lived in for more than four years. Jackson swept his gaze over her. Shock pervaded it and something else.

Pushing his laptop onto the sofa, he shot up and walked toward her. And Clio automatically stepped back.

Do not betray yourself, bella.

With Stefan's warning ringing in her ears, she forced herself to not flinch as Jackson neared her. Her gut twisted and she wondered if Stefan had been right. That she was not up to even facing Jackson again.

"Clio?"

At five-nine, she topped him a good couple of inches. His gaze on level with hers, he cupped her cheek. There was no way to curb the shiver that spewed within.

"Is everything all right?"

The false sweetness in his greeting sent nausea rising through her. "Actually, I'm not okay."

There was no need to pretend about her mood. She had not an ounce of belief that she could carry it off even if she tried.

Stepping away from him, she walked to the refrigerator and grabbed a bottle of water.

His gaze was still on her but she let hers drift over the sitting area and the dining room.

Desperate to be loved, desperate to feel she's succeeded at something...

Her chest was so tight that it felt like a miracle that she was breathing. Because everywhere she looked, there was no trace of her in the space she had lived in for four years. It was all either an extension of Jackson's loud personality or the abode of a New York financier. Nothing about the flat reflected her.

How had she not seen this until now? Her fingers shaking on the plastic bottle, she took a sip of the water and forced the knot in her throat down.

"Clio, you left the party yesterday without informing me, you didn't return last night except for that text. Where the hell were you?"

"With an old friend," she replied, finally setting her gaze on him.

Not one strand of his expertly cut blond hair was out of place. He was dressed to impress in a charcoal-gray suit—his ice-blue shirt chosen explicitly to bring out the blue of his eyes by none other than Ashley and picked up at the dry cleaner every week by Clio.

He had screwed his assistant barely half a mile away from her and had the temerity to demand explanation of her. Felt not an ounce of shame or guilt. Not even a shadow of hesitation.

Had she made it that easy for him? Had it been so easy to mock her, to use her?

"Clio... Open that mouth and say something or—"

"Or what, Jackson?" the question burst out of her on a wave of anger. Closing her eyes, she took a deep breath and counted to ten.

The minute Stefan had shown her into the extra bedroom, she had collapsed onto the bed. Yet, sleep had evaded her, the awareness she had tried so hard to shove away descending on her. She pressed her fingers against her temple. "I don't feel good."

Instantly, Jackson's expression fell, like a little boy who was on the verge of a tantrum. "Don't tell me you have another headache coming on. Really, Clio, you would think you would have enough sense to know what triggers one of your episodes... It's damned inconvenient of you to be getting one every time we have something important going on."

Perversely, Jackson's sheer lack of concern filled Clio's throat with tears more than his cheating. "I do not plan them, Jackson."

"Is that why you walked away last night while Jane and I waited? You knew how important that meeting was to me."

"I was ill for two weeks, Jackson. A concept you don't seem to understand because you dragged me there even after I told you so. While you were gallivanting around the world, I was here alone, sick with flu. I had barely recovered when you stormed in here and asked me to get ready for that dinner."

A curse flew from his mouth and he almost shoved the cordless phone in her face. "Fine. Pop some pills. Call Jane Alcott, in the next few minutes. Make another appointment. And then call the Savoy and book a table for tomorrow's lunch, I want this deal with Jane done. Like yesterday. And make sure you sound cheery.

"The old biddy asked me a hundred questions after you left last night. Looked at me as though I was responsible for your headaches. And half the time I can't even understand what the bloody hell she's saying."

"God, show her some respect, Jackson."

He glanced at her with such obvious disbelief that Clio cringed inwardly. Was he so shocked at even the smallest sign of an angry response from her?

"What is wrong with you? You have this crazed look in your eyes. God, you're not pregnant, are you, Clio?"

"How could I be when you haven't touched me in four months?"

The minute she said it, Clio blinked.

Was it any wonder he had walked all over her? The very way she had framed her question meant she had given all her power to him. Every aspect of their relationship had been his to rule.

Something close to shame crossed his face. Would he apologize? Would he make an excuse? Her heart rising to her throat, Clio waited with bated breath. And hated herself a little more for the fact that she did.

"That's not my fault, is it?" he said, his gaze shying away from hers. And something monumental crumbled inside Clio. If there could be a sound for despondence, it would be the sound that she caught in her throat.

"Half the time, you're unhappy with yourself, half the time, you are unhappy with me. And you have a hundred hang-ups about sex. For Christ's sake, Clio, sex is not always about cuddling, and sharing dreams and words of love. Sex should sometimes be just bloody sex. Nothing wrong with letting go in bed. But you can never do that, can you?"

"Do you not care at all about how I feel, Jackson?" The pitiful question left her mouth before Clio knew she was asking it. The desperation in her tone tied with the almost hopeful note made bile rise in her throat.

It was like watching an alternate version of herself talking to Jackson, hoping he would give an answer that would fix everything she had heard last night, as if it could magically erase the ugliness of their relationship.

That infinitesimal sliver of hope was the most pathetic thing she had ever seen in her life.

I don't trust you to not crawl back to him while I'm gone.

Stefan's word pricked her and she turned away from Jackson.

Everything inside her shook, everything inside her

wanted to fall apart and give in to the maelstrom of grief swirling within. But she couldn't. Not yet.

Squaring her shoulders, she turned around and let the years of breeding that she had turned back on slide into place. She had been taught by the best nannies in England about holding her own even when the world around her was in chaos.

"I can't call Jane today. I don't have time."

"Why the hell not?"

"I'm leaving for Athens. I have a hundred things to do before that."

"Athens, Greece?"

A brittle smile curved her mouth. "Yes, Athens, Greece. Christian Markos's wedding won't happen in any other place, I'm thinking."

"Christian Markos? *The* Christian Markos? You're invited to his wedding?" The light that came on in Jackson's face was unlike anything she had ever seen. His suddenly positive energy and the smile that he flashed at her added another layer of ice around her heart.

She meant nothing to him. Even though she had known it, the truth left her shaking.

"Why have you never mentioned that you were acquainted with him?"

"I'm not just acquainted with him. Christian is a very close friend."

"That's even more fantastic." He grabbed the phone and dialed a number, Ashley's she was sure.

Clio grabbed the phone from him just as Ashley said hello and clicked it off. "You're not invited, Jackson."

What had she ever seen in him, Clio wondered. How had she fooled herself so thoroughly when everything about him was so much artifice?

"You will need a plus one. And who else will you bring but me? It's not like you have a whole lot of friends other than mine."

Because she had built her entire life around him.

"I'm bringing no one. Christian and my other friends are—"

"What other friends?"

"Rocco Mondelli, Zayed Al Afzal and—" her throat clenched "—Stefan Bianco. The media is fond of calling them—"

"The Columbia Four," he finished with a hungry gleam in his eyes.

Clio could almost hear his mental gears clicking, could see her pitiful place in his life extend for a few more months while Ashley gave birth to his child.

"Do you know all of them really well? Even that arrogant Sicilian, Bianco?"

"Yes," Clio said, every nerve in her stretched tight. "Stefan is a friend, too." She forced a smile to her lips and crossed her arms. "All four of them are insanely protective of their private lives and I don't want to impose on them."

He ran a blunt-tipped finger over his brow, his gaze assessing her. "It's not the right time for you to be leaving New York, Clio. Cancel this trip. I need you here to finish signing on as Jane's financier and then there's…"

Clio shook her head, her gut twisting at the way he instantly changed tactics. "It's what you said when Rocco got married, too. I let you browbeat me into missing the most important day in the life of one of my oldest friends. I have a life, too, Jackson."

"Do you?"

"Yes," she whispered, not liking the look in his eyes. "One that I have forgotten exists these past years."

"Fine. Go to Athens. Do your socializing and networking. And when you come back, we'll have a little chat about Stefan Bianco. That man's been in a thorn in my side for too long."

The minute Jackson left, Clio's legs gave out from under

her. She sank to the thick carpet, the pristine white walls closing in on her.

Telling herself that she had gotten through the hardest part, she took a deep breath.

She turned on his laptop, then picked herself up and wandered into Jackson's study, looking in his cabinets and drawers. Her heart thudded in her chest but she knew he wouldn't come back tonight.

There was nothing to salvage in her relationship with Jackson. He had trampled her heart and shattered her trust.

Clio shuddered and typed in the password to their company's database, wondering if she would ever be whole again.

CHAPTER FIVE

CLIO LOOKED AROUND the ancient structure of the Parthenon and felt a measure of peace she hadn't felt in a long time.

Christian's wedding last night had been the most beautiful ceremony she had seen in a while.

Deciding to walk the short distance from the luxury hotel to view the ancient ruins up close was the best decision she had made.

The lunch on the terrace this afternoon with Rocco and Olivia, Zayed, Christian and his new bride Alessandra, and Stefan, had begun so well. She had felt like she was among friends.

Olivia had asked so many questions about when the four men and she had been at Columbia together over a decade ago, and Clio had regaled them with stories, glad to fill the brooding silence with chatter.

Until the discussion had turned to Clio's own life.

What had Clio been up to all these years? Was Clio involved with anyone?

They had all been only polite questions from people who were interested in her life. But what did she have to tell them?

Turning around, she clicked a couple more pictures with her digital camera, marveled anew.

Her raised hand stilled as she saw the tall, wide frame of Stefan coming close. June sun shone behind him, leaving his defined face in shadows. His paper-thin white cotton shirt was buffeted against his broad frame, tapering against his waist. Even though he couldn't see her, Clio dragged her gaze away from following down. She didn't need to see his powerful thighs encased in jeans.

The whipcord tightness of his muscles, the tensile strength of his legs, the wide swathe of his shoulders and the way they narrowed down her world to him, she had noticed far too much of him already on their flight to Athens. The sheer luxury and scale of his private jet, which she'd learned was the closest thing to a home for him, had rendered her mute. But it was the man himself who had occupied her mind all through the flight.

All the while she had been packing for the trip, all through the limo ride to the private airstrip where he had been waiting, it had been easy to tell herself that she would see this through.

She still wanted to. Because what Jackson had done had poisoned her so much that she couldn't look at her own reflection in the mirror without wanting to shatter it into a million shards.

It was the man she had gone to, to accomplish her revenge who continually disconcerted her.

Stefan had been nothing but courteous and concerned on the flight, if a bit preoccupied. And yet every time their gazes met or they accidentally touched, the moment arched and stretched, a latent energy pulsed until one of them looked away, or stepped back.

It was the last thing Clio wanted to face.

He came to a halt about a foot from her, watching her.

Feeling compelled to break the intense silence, she waved her hands around. "I can't believe Christian obtained private and uncurtailed access to the Parthenon, of all places. Even I'm impressed by this show of power and status. Does Alessandra mean so much to him, then?"

For once, she was glad that there was no wistful note in her tone. Only open curiosity.

Stefan shrugged, a cold light in his eyes. It was like there was frost all around them even as the sun cast long shadows. "If Alessandra was the kind to be impressed by this, it would make sense. For all the success he has achieved, Christian has a chip on his shoulder about where he started in life.

"He doesn't realize yet that Alessandra is one of those rare women who care nothing about his wealth or status."

Clio blinked. It was her casual comment that a woman would be impressed by the power that clung to the Columbia Four that had made him look so coldly forbidding.

Did he still think of Serena, the woman who had so blithely broken his heart? Did he think all women were like her, that Clio was like her?

Of course he did, Clio realized. And she had only confirmed his view by going to him for help, by suggesting that she wanted to use that very power and status as her shield.

She couldn't begin to care about Stefan's opinion. Not when it was decided already, not when her self-esteem was in such tatters.

"Is he in love with her, do you think?" she said, turning her mind away from what lay ahead.

"I would have said no. But I have changed my opinion about Rocco and Olivia, so who knows?" He tucked his hands into his pockets and took a few more steps. "I didn't realize running away was a habit of yours."

The bland smile falling from her face, Clio looked up. "I don't know what you mean."

"You did it that night at the Empire State Building instead of confronting that jerk. You did it today."

"I did…no such thing."

"Olivia said you looked like you were having an anxiety attack. She was concerned for you, just as I was." There was almost a fond note in his tone for Rocco's wife. "Why did you leave?"

"There seems to be a lot of friction between Christian and Rocco."

"Rocco will need time to forgive Christian for tangling with his little sister. But the fact that he is here shows how much Alessandra means to him."

"I felt like I was intruding."

"Zayed and I were right there."

"You are a part of each other's lives. Rocco and Christian need your support to get through this rough patch. I'm little more than a stranger."

"No. You and I know very well that you were actually a good buffer back there. Those stories you had of the four of us from Columbia made everyone laugh. Everyone took a collective breath."

He reached her and tugged her hand into his. Instant charge crackled around them.

"You said the female students at Columbia used to be supremely envious of you and at the same time sugared you up so that they could get a tidbit about one of us. What did you call yourself?"

She had felt his gaze on her like a physical caress all through the lunch. Now it disconcerted her to know that he remembered every word she had said. The intensity of his attention kept her wondering what about her interested him so. "The Gateway to the Columbia Four."

He smiled at that and warmth filled his gaze. "Rocco has been like a mad bull all this time but even he cracked a smile there. Then you were gone. I thought you had bolted."

"And where would I go? By bringing me here aboard your private jet, you made sure I had nowhere to go except with you. You even had them unpack my stuff and take my passport. Do not manipulate me, Stefan."

Ice coated his words. "I was doing it for your own good."

Clio couldn't back down. If she didn't take a stand now, she never would. Their relationship or the facade of it, was a temporary one. But still, she wanted to set the right tone for it.

Never again would she let her sense of identity be lost in a man.

"Don't presume to know it better than me."

"But isn't that what love-struck fiancés do, *bella*? Cater to your every need and whim? Cosset you in luxuries and act possessive? Know what's good for you better than yourself?"

Clio flinched, the ease with which he used her history to make his point cruelly efficient.

The hardness didn't budge from his expression. "We're supposed to be falling in love even now. You think the world will buy that Stefan Bianco let his almost-intended fly economy on a commercial airline?"

"Maybe the world will think that Stefan Bianco finally met a woman who doesn't fall at his feet?" she retorted, lifting her chin.

He smiled and ran a finger over her chin, a thoughtful expression on his face.

"How come you have no trouble putting me in place, *bella*?" Moving closer, he laid his hands on her bare shoulders and turned her toward the terrace. "Do you know how you looked from the terrace, Clio?"

Not trusting that she could find her voice, Clio shook her head. Even with the sun shining above them, the heat of his body behind her was like a caress.

She should move away, she knew. Stop him from continuing, at least. Cut this line of conversation before it began.

There was no space for personal observations or shared experiences between them. There was nothing but a common, twisted goal. But something in the honeyed tone of his voice locked the words in her throat.

His finger landed on her chin and tilted it up, facing away from the sun.

"Shall I tell you?"

He was taunting her. He knew that she was standing on

the precipice of retreating. He was daring her, even as he was certain of her cowardice.

She had read that the Parthenon had served as a church, a mosque, even a munitions depot during the Turkish occupation of Greece.

Yet there it stood today, majestic, beautiful, a monument to one of the greatest civilizations of the world.

And she, she was afraid of hearing one man's opinion of her. Was afraid of even facing the truth that was in his eyes.

Everything about her life was in ruins just like the Parthenon. But she decided to take the chance. Just for that moment, she would choose to be unafraid. She would pretend she had become the woman she wanted to be when she had set out for Columbia University.

She would pretend that when a man like Stefan Bianco looked at her, there was not resigned concern or eviscerating censure at what she had done to her life. But admiration and respect... The way he had looked at her once.

The base of his palm was hard and unyielding against her lower back. Her skin burned with every ridge and line leaving an imprint on her skin.

Turning toward him, she met his gaze, fighting the urge to pull away and to run far. "Tell me how I looked, Stefan."

The green of his eyes widened just a bit. That she had surprised him, she clutched it to her like a reward for her bravery.

"With that cream dress only covering one shoulder, your hair flying behind you, the sun turning your skin golden, you looked like the goddess Athena herself. For a few seconds, you had me stunned. And it has been a while since I let myself believe in any kind of myth."

Bitter laughter spilled from Clio's mouth and got lost in the vastness around her. "Goddess Athena was supposed to have been fierce and brave. I'm nothing like her, Stefan." Turning away from him, she sighed. "You were right. I ran away from the terrace because I couldn't breathe there."

"Why?"

"Let it go, Stefan."

"No."

"Haven't you seen enough? Won't you leave me with even a facade to hide behind?"

"No, I won't. Better me than the whole world, *bella*, than the corrupt man you left behind. Jackson won't meekly accept our engagement. There's only going to be more—"

"Light on me, yeah? I know."

How pathetic was she that for a minute she'd thought he insisted because he cared. How easily she fell into her own trap of wanting to matter...

She was nothing but a means to an end for Stefan. Just as she had been to Jackson. Only with Stefan, there were no lies, no deception.

"I saw Olivia Fitzgerald, the supermodel. I saw Alessandra Mondelli, world-famous photographer. Every woman who was in there was someone who had made a life for herself in the world, someone who carved a niche for what she exceled in. Then I caught my reflection in the jug. Who'd think a jug could do so much for you, right?"

And both women, while beautiful and successful, had men who respected them and loved them.

"Here I was sitting among some of the most accomplished women on the planet and what did I have to show for a decade of slogging, for a lifetime of walking away from a safe life...

"Nothing.

"I couldn't stay another minute and puncture the happiness of so many people. I couldn't forgive myself if I did that.

"Do you still see the goddess Athena, Stefan?"

His fingers tightened on her bare arms, his face fierce as he looked down at her. "You walked away from him. By your own words, you crawled out from the lowest point of your life and came to me. And you had enough guts to use what you saw in my face that night to your own advantage.

"I know what it takes to move ahead from that moment in which your heart shatters and there's nothing but a hole in your chest.

"All you need to do now is stay the course and carve your life the way you want. And until you can wage your own battle, I'll do it for you."

His words were whispers that reverberated around them in the open space.

Clio nodded slowly.

For all the ruthlessness that had become second skin to him, Stefan was much kinder than a mirror. When she looked in his eyes, her own reflection held promise. Touched by a brave past that she had almost forgotten, it held hope.

He was using her and she was using him. It was the perfect relationship for two people who had been burned by love, who had had their hearts shattered and trodden upon.

A man who would love her unconditionally—she didn't even know what that meant anymore. Maybe she had never deserved it.

But she so much wanted that day when she wouldn't run away in shame, when she wouldn't feel this cavernous emptiness inside at another woman's success.

The day when she wasn't an utter failure in life.

She sketched a bow in front of him, letting hope fill her entire body.

"Then I'm ready for training, Master."

A matching smile curved his mouth and he returned her bow and then stepped back into an elaborate pose that had economic movements and slices through the air that were perfectly synchronous. "Let us begin, Clio."

Shaking her head, Clio laughed. For anyone watching them from the hotel, they would look comical.

"If you tell me you're like a black belt in karate or some such thing, I'll have to knock your teeth in, Bianco. I can only take so much of your all-rounded macho perfection before I start choking on it."

Grooves bracketed his serious mouth as he burst into laughter. With his hair falling onto his forehead, his stunning features bathed in sunlight, he looked like one of those warriors that could have conquered the Parthenon.

"All-rounded macho perfection?" he said, color bleeding into those sculpted cheeks.

Narrowing her eyes, Clio stepped toward him. "Let me look at you," she mumbled, laughter bubbling up inside her. He shielded his face with his forearm and she pulled it down.

"Oh. My. God. You're blushing." She lifted her camera and clicked close-ups of him and he tried to grab it from her. Pushing back at his chest with one hand, which was like an impenetrable wall, she clicked some more.

She swung the camera away from him, still laughing. "There's my fortune. Women of the world are going to be crazy for it. A shot of arrogant Sicilian Stefan Bianco doing something as mundane and human as blushing."

A vein flickered in his temple, his mouth tight with laughter. "Stop it, *bella*."

"Oh, come on. Like you don't know your own appeal. Why do you think that model went nuts over you dumping her?"

"The regular gifts she was ordering for herself from Tiffany's? The champagne and caviar and the trips to Paris and London and Hong Kong aboard my private jet? The modeling contracts she was getting offered by networking through me?"

The camera dangling from her raised hand, Clio went still.

He had become so cynical, she remembered Christian saying a few years after they had left Columbia. But to see that hardness become such an intrinsic part of him that he filtered everything in the world through that, it was such a sharp contrast to the man she had known.

Did he think there was nothing about him, the true him, that would appeal to a genuine woman? Or had he made it true by burying everything that had been so intrinsically good about him?

"You don't believe that of all of them, do you, Stefan?"

"Of course not. Let's not forget my masculine prowess," he added with a wink that in no way belied the cold truth in his eyes.

Clio rolled her eyes and swatted his forearm, hiding the shiver that went through her.

"I'll reduce my *awesomeness* into little doses for you, *si*?" His English favored a stronger accent just then. "I know that you're going all...*fluttery* inside—" he moved his hand in front of himself, encompassing his lean frame "—at the thought of having me all to yourself."

More laughter spilled from her mouth as forgotten memories of him making a play for her at Columbia during that first year rushed forth. His attentions were almost a knee-jerk response to any moderately attractive woman.

Oh, she had had so much fun cutting him down to size every time he had tried it during that first year. Had missed the chance to put him down after he had fallen in love with Serena, though.

"Okay, that's it, Bianco. You need to be pegged down a bit."

His hands on his hips, his lush lower lip jutting out, he stared her down. "And you're the woman for it, Norwood?"

Tingles swept through her at his open challenge, mocking as it was. "Of course I am. If not for me cutting you down to size, you would have grown a second head back when we were at uni."

He grinned. "I do have a second head—"

Blushing and laughing, Clio clapped her hand over his mouth. Sharp teeth dug into the heel of her palm and she squealed.

Her tummy felt tight and achy, and tears ran down her

face as he chased her and she ran, both of them hurling long forgotten challenges at each other.

How long had it been since she had laughed like this?

He had just caught her when they heard the whir of rotor blades.

The sound fractured the moment so effectively that she flinched. Instantly, Stefan pulled her behind him. Shocked at how low the chopper was flying and the long-range camera directed toward the terrace, Clio clutched Stefan's shirt and hid her face in his muscled back.

A pithy curse fell from his mouth.

"Is this all so that they can have a story on Alessandra?" she asked, remembering the scandal that had haunted Rocco's sister.

"Yes. But they won't get anything on her as long as I have something to say about it."

Her heart raced as the muscles of his back tensed under her fingers. "How? Even you can't sprout wings and block the chopper."

His arm shot out and pulled her forward. Tripping against her own feet, she fell onto Stefan. And jerked at the sudden male heat that surrounded her. His arm around her waist was like a muscular rope she couldn't pry off her.

Warmth crawled up all over her body, the scent of him swirling around her, binding her to him.

"No, I can't sprout wings, *bella*." Slumberous heat came alive in his gaze. "But I have a beautiful woman next to me and I can give the hounds a juicier piece of meat first. By the time they're through with us, Christian will have his own security armed and Alessandra protected from the worst of it."

Realizing too late what he intended, Clio pushed away from his chest. "No, Stefan. There has to be another way."

But he was as solid and impenetrable as the walls of the Parthenon. He clasped her face with his palms, and tilted it up toward him.

"Look at me, *bella*. Pretend like you can't get enough of me."

She didn't have to pretend. The errant thought stole through her, inciting a panic. She didn't have to pretend that she was already flailing, falling into the haze he cast over her senses with ease.

She struggled again and their legs tangled, the tensile, hard muscles of his thighs rubbing against hers.

The sound of his jagged exhale settled over her skin, while the whir of the rotor blades of the chopper above felt like a death knell.

Her breath left Clio in a dizzying whoosh, every inch of her thrumming and pulsing. "Wait...I..."

Words melted away from Clio's lips as the pad of his thumb moved over her chin, traced the curve of her lower lip. "It's just one kiss, *bella*. If you flinch every time I lay a finger on you, no one's going to buy it, Clio. Least of all Jackson."

Her breath hitched like a balloon inside her, crushing her chest with a weight she couldn't bear... The last thing she wanted was a kiss and that, too, from the man who could so easily shred the small part of her that was still intact.

But the reminder didn't work quite as well as it should have.

Because when he dipped his head and touched her lips, Clio felt her own walls tremble and quake, her skin burn with need and fire, felt the shudder that racked his wide, solid frame.

His lips were rough and soft, his jaw bristly against her skin, and his thick eyelashes not hiding his shocked expression for once.

"Cristo, bella," he whispered, touching his forehead to hers.

His nose rubbed against hers, a strange intimacy growing around them.

"Stefan," she begged, desperate to flee, but yearning to

feel that rough mouth against hers again. Desperate to be touched again, desperate to feel his muscles tense. "Don't do this."

His fingers crawled over her nape and into her hair, his gaze almost angry. "I can't stop, Clio. Not now."

He slanted his mouth over hers and dragged it across.

Fiery need burst across the seam of her lips and Clio shuddered all over.

With a curse that resounded in the air, Stefan tightened his grip until her scalp prickled. Buried his nose in the crook of her neck and breathed.

"You smell like sunshine and oranges, *bella*. *Dio*, you taste like..."

Clio didn't know what else he said. All the fight left her as he found her mouth again and devoured it with little bites and nips. Stroked and tasted her lips as if she was a feast to be savored.

Kissed her as if there was nothing else he wanted to do, as if nothing but her total surrender would do.

And Clio surrendered. To him and even more, to the desire inside her, both freeing and binding.

Their bodies fused to each other as they crossed a line they shouldn't have.

A kiss they could never undo because it already engulfed them.

A day later, Clio and he were due to leave for New York in a couple of hours and the chasm of need that the kiss had ripped open felt just as raw to Stefan.

He had only meant the kiss as an evasion.

But one taste of her lush, pink, trembling mouth, and he had been knocked in the gut. All of the fantasies he had spun around her as a raging twenty-year-old became intoxicating reality.

Prowling the carpeted interior of his suite, he stared at the video coverage of the kiss that was already being aired on every site that fed on his life, his mood slowly spiraling out of his control.

Just as his libido did by the memories of her warm mouth, the scent of her skin, of the way she had shuddered and moaned when he tangled his tongue with hers.

Watching their kiss shouldn't have been the most erotic experience he had ever had. Exhaling a pent-up breath, he acknowledged it was.

Christian and Alessandra's wedding and reception had gone on without an ugly visit from the media, thanks to his diversionary tactics. But there was a betrayed look in Clio's eyes that pierced him when she met his gaze now.

Like he had crossed an imaginary boundary between them.

And the fact that he could think of nothing but baring her completely to him, of removing the fear and self-doubt that had flashed in her eyes and replacing it with liquid lust, proved her right.

It had been a long time since a kiss had turned him inside out with need.

A long time since anything had touched him.

But he would have preferred if it had been anyone but her.

The short clip was already up on most celebrity gossip websites and spreading like a virus. The rabid speculation had begun.

His features had been distinctive. So the media knew it was him.

What they hadn't figured out yet was her identity. And they were going crazy trying to figure out who the new woman in his life was, angling to find out who else was on the guest list at Christian's wedding.

The press had dubbed her Bianco's Redhead, a name he was sure the redhead in question was going to dislike, if not despise.

He grabbed the remote just as Rocco, wearing the blackest scowl Stefan had ever seen, entered the suite without knocking.

His gaze turned to the plasma screen on the far wall seconds before Stefan turned it off. The silence grew heavy, almost stifling, as Rocco, his oldest friend, studied him.

"Whatever you want to say, don't," Stefan snarled, his hackles rising at his friend's continued silence.

"All four of us have treated the world and the women in it as our playground for years, true," Rocco said, cutting straight to the point, "but I always thought there was still a bit of honor left in all of us. First Christian with Lessie, and now you and Clio... *Dio*, didn't you find anyone else to play with other than our oldest friend, Stefan?"

Stefan had had every intention of telling his friends the utter truth. But now, his friend's well-meaning interference locked the words in his throat. Even as the short clip was sweeping the internet like wildfire for all the world to see, to actually dissect their kiss with Rocco, to reveal Clio's confidence and their deal, felt too private.

Too intimate to be shared.

Which in itself should have rung all his internal alarms like a damn gong.

He ran the heel of his palm against his jaw, striving for a casual tone. One kiss and it was like Mount Etna had erupted.

"I'm not playing with her."

"No? In a decade, I have not seen you make one meaningful connection with another person, much less a woman. And you always had a thing for her. Damn it, you cannot play with and then discard Clio like you—"

"Enough, Rocco," he said through gritted teeth.

Leashing his temper by the skin of his teeth, because no way did he want to betray how much that kiss had affected him, Stefan smiled at Rocco. "Just because you have settled into marital bliss with Olivia doesn't mean you can expect us all to change colors already, *fratello*. Clio…she is safe from me."

Grinning, Rocco clapped him on the back. And once again, Stefan wondered at how well love and Olivia suited Rocco.

He had never seen his friend so happy and at peace.

"You know I had to—"

"Not needed, Rocco," Stefan said.

Rocco looked at him as if he wanted to say something more. Instead, he embraced Stefan and bid him goodbye.

Pouring himself a drink, Stefan went to the balcony.

Olivia and Clio were seated at the outdoor café on the ground floor.

Instantly Stefan shifted to see Clio better. She wasn't laughing like Olivia but a smile curved her mouth. And something loosened in his chest.

He was glad she was smiling again. She had lost that awful pallor, that stricken, lost look she had had when she had come to his suite.

As if she could sense his eyes on her, she looked up.

Across the distance, their gazes held. Stefan raised his glass and she did the same with a nod.

The elegant set of her shoulders, the long fiery locks, the high cheekbones—everything about her drew his attention.

With a ruthless will, he pulled his gaze away from her and went back into his suite.

He couldn't touch her again, couldn't risk any complications. Women and sex were uncomplicated for him. It was the only way he had put himself together, the only way he had moved forward after Serena's betrayal.

Clio, whatever state she was in, deserved a hell of lot more. He had nothing to give her except memories of what she had been, except to be her pretend strength to face a man he abhorred.

The only reason he had agreed to this was because he

needed justice to be served for Marco. He needed her help to see through Jackson's destruction.

Switching his phone on, he made a call to his PR guy and to his head of security, instructing him to leak her name as the woman in the clip.

The sooner they accomplished what they had come together for, the sooner Clio would be out of his life, untouched and unscathed.

CHAPTER SIX

THEY WERE JUST an hour away from landing in a private airstrip in New York. Finally, Clio gathered enough nerve to switch on her tablet and opened a search engine.

More than once, her fingers slipped on the smooth surface. Tension turned her shoulders into stiff rods as she finally typed Stefan's name.

Because he would be at the center of all this, he was the one whose coattails she would be riding through the storm they were unleashing.

Her heart hammered in her throat as the video file played again and she saw Stefan's body enveloping her protectively even as they were lost in each other.

It spoke to the man she had known once.

Closing the video file, she scrolled down and froze at the title.

Bianco's Redhead Is None Other than Clio Norwood, New York Financier Jackson Smith's Fiancée of Three Years.

There was no end to the questions posed, to the number of links to other articles. No end to how the media talked about it as though it was a win on Stefan's part that he had landed her. As though she was a prize and not a woman with feelings and emotions.

How did Stefan Bianco steal Clio Norwood from under the nose of Jackson Smith?

How long has the affair been going on? Is it serious?

Which Man Will Clio Norwood Choose in the End? one

headline read, giving Clio at least the illusion of power over her own choices.

Even having been prepared for it, anger, disbelief and frustration and so many more emotions ran through Clio.

Bianco's Redhead... God!

Clio laughed so hard that her jaw hurt, her eyes pooled. She took the tissue that Stefan patiently extended and wiped her face.

There was a relief in realizing she had seen the worst, and lived to tell it.

Stefan gazed at her with a stunned expression in his eyes. "Clio, why you are smiling?"

Clio pointed to the tablet and shrugged. "Bianco's Blonde has so much more zing, don't you think?" She fingered her hair and pulled it forward. "Maybe I will dye it."

Leaning forward in a movement that jammed the breath in her throat, he caught the thick strands between his fingers, a reverent expression in his gaze. Instant tension wove around them, thick and charged.

"No, *bella*," he said, his words a rough command that would brook no argument.

Wrapping the silky locks around two of his fingers, he turned them around and around, tugging her forward.

There was a feral quality to his gaze as it turned to her, a possessiveness that drenched her in heat. "Do not dare to change a strand of it, Clio. Whatever transformation you think you need, I forbid you to ruin something so glorious."

The sight of his hair-roughened wrists handling her hair sent a tremor through her. As did the inherent command in his tone. There was nothing about him that didn't cause Clio to lose her breath, that didn't make her feel as though she would combust if he didn't touch her.

But if he did, if she let him explore this heat between them, as every tingling inch of her wanted to, there would be nothing left.

And his eviscerating brand of friendship was the only precious thing left to her.

"We can't keep doing this, Stefan," she said, her words hoarse and uneven, completely opposite to how she wanted to sound. "I…can't think straight when you touch me and I need everything I have to deal with Jackson."

The magnitude of her admission hung in the air around them but she would rather face the attraction between them than pretend it wasn't always there.

Slowly, he unwound his fingers around her hair. Disappointment and fury wreathed his features until inch by inch, he pushed them out of his face. "How do you suggest we pretend to be engaged without touching each other, Clio? If you're weak enough to call the thing off because you can't—"

"I don't think it's weak to acknowledge a weakness." She held his gaze steadily. "To pretend in front of the world and even our friends, it's one thing. But I don't want anything else to muddy our relationship."

"It worked perfectly for us this time, but it won't happen again, *sì*."

Rubbing a hand over her tummy, Clio nodded jerkily.

When he met her gaze again, it was impassive, in control. And Clio almost bought it. But now that she had tasted the heat of his kiss, saw him smile and argue with Rocco, she knew it was only a hardened facade.

Stefan still felt as passionately as he had done a decade ago. Only now, all that firestorm of emotion and passion was buried under a coldly ruthless will.

And it twisted her gut that that well of passion, all that love he had to give, would never see the light of day again.

His ready acceptance suddenly threw her even though it was what she wanted. What she needed.

"Anything else, Clio?"

"I won't be made a fool of again, Stefan. Not even in a pretend relationship."

"I do not understand."

Heat crept up her neck and she pointed to the tablet, images of him with other women accompanied with captions like *predatory playboy* in capital letters.

Stefan changed girlfriends like she did her clothes. And their kiss, it had made her feel more alive than she had in years.

Two different facts and both she needed to accept without giving it more weight.

"You are never without a woman."

Something devilish gleamed in his gaze. "You still have me lost, *bella*. Say it in words I can understand, Clio. You forget that English is not my language."

She was not a prude. But thinking of Stefan and sex in the same sentence sent a burst of heat through her belly that she didn't even begin to know how to handle.

He knew how uncomfortable she was talking about this and yet he was goading her.

"What are you going to do for sex, Bianco?" she said, gritting her jaw, daring him to laugh at her now.

He did it anyway, but it was an indulgent smile that cut grooves through his cheeks. Her fingers itched to trace them, to feel the stubble on his cheek.

"Was that so hard?"

"No." She returned his smile, feeling as if they were on equal footing again. "You haven't answered me, though."

"I will not *take up* a woman on the side while all this is going on, *sì*? You have my word, *bella*. And I'm sure a few months of deprivation won't kill me. If I do get desperate, I have two very capable hands," he said, holding them up, his expression deadpan.

Blushing at how quickly her mind supplied an image of him, naked, Clio threw her purse at him. "Too much information, Bianco."

He waggled his brows at her and, shaking her head at that lewd expression, she laughed.

"You have such a beautiful laugh, Clio. You should do it more."

Struck speechless by his abrupt observation, Clio nodded.

"We'll be landing in an hour," he said, tilting his head toward the New York skyline emerging through the clouds and visible through the windows. "Have you started looking at Jackson's documents? Do you require help?"

"No, I can do it myself," Clio replied, just hearing Jackson's name making her feel dirty from the inside. "I have downloaded and printed every document pertaining to his finances and his hedge fund company. There isn't a single number or transaction that I don't have a hard copy of. But I haven't seen anything yet, Stefan. Are you sure—"

"He's dirty? Yes. I'll bet my entire fortune on that."

Leaning back against the seat, he propped one ankle over the other knee. Clasped his hands behind his head, causing his white dress shirt to stretch tight against that wide chest. "Keep looking, *bella*."

"It's fascinating. For example, did you know that when—"

"So you *still* have a thing for numbers," he drawled softly.

"And you're still the only man in the world that can make that sound dirty."

"Now that you have me locked in with no relief in sight, I have to find my pleasure where I can," he said with a twinkle in his eye.

Clio looked away from him, feeling the heat of his gaze like a caress, praying that she didn't fall apart before she had a chance to be whole again.

Because this time there would not even be pieces of her heart and self-respect left.

Leaning forward, he tugged her left hand into his. She barely managed a gasp as the diamond ring slid in smooth and cold against her skin.

Her heart slammed against her rib cage. Instant refusal

rose to her lips. But she held it off as she caught Stefan's expression.

Distaste, and something else, something she didn't even want to know, glimmered in his eyes.

Was he remembering Serena just as she was thinking of Jackson?

That day in the flat, she had removed the heavy, over-the-top diamond that Jackson had bought for her. Had finally felt free after so long.

Eyeing the ring, she willed herself to calm down. This was only a pretense, something she was walking into with her head screwed on right.

At least it was something that was close to her own taste—the most beautifully cut diamond, in a princess setting.

Her gaze flew to Stefan, who watched her with an intensity that arrested her thought process.

"Stefan, thank you…for everything. I—"

"Not required, *bella*. Do not, even for a moment, believe I'm doing you a favor or that there's anything personal to all this. You have your side of the bargain and I have mine to keep up."

While she grappled with his ruthless warning, he leaned forward and unbuckled her belt. "We will see Jackson tonight at a party, Clio. I made sure he can't get to you before the evening. But obviously he will be foaming at the mouth to see you and to challenge me. He will make a scene, *bella*, and if I'm right about Jackson, it's going to get dirty.

"Do you have what it takes to face him, Clio?"

"And if I don't want to?"

"Then I will drag you with me anyway. Jackson needs to be stopped and I won't get an opportunity like this again."

The utter ruthlessness with which he said it stunned Clio. Every time she thought she knew him, he surprised her again. Once again, she wondered why Stefan despised Jackson so much.

But with a self-preservation instinct she should have had long before this, she didn't prod him. For some reason, understanding what drove Stefan was a territory she didn't want to go into. So she reassured him of her own intentions. "I'll never want him back in my life, Stefan. This week has helped me see more than just Jackson's betrayal.

"I'll need you to stand by me tonight, but yes, I'm ready to take Jackson on."

For once, there were no doubts in his gaze as it swept over her face searchingly. And Clio measured her progress in that green gaze, felt a small flicker of hope for herself.

"You have me, *bella*. For as long as you want."

The moment Stefan helped her out of the limo onto the private estate in the Hamptons where the night's party was, Clio heard the exponential rise in the intensity of the charged atmosphere.

Flashes of cameras and microphones were thrust in their faces from behind ropes. Their names seemed like a chant on a hundred lips.

Jackson had always been a media favorite, too.

Handsome, hardworking, successful—the perfect poster boy for America's success stories. Or at least that was the image he had liked to project.

But the crowd that the security team was trying to corral tonight was like nothing Jackson had ever warranted.

Clutching the ring on her finger like a lifeline, Clio fisted and unfisted her hands as security guards ushered them inside the mansion through the throng.

"Mr. Bianco, are you seeing Ms. Norwood now?"

"Ms. Norwood, is it true you and Mr. Bianco were college sweethearts at Columbia?"

"Have you left Jackson Smith for Mr. Bianco? Or is it his bigger and better status and wealth that lured you in?"

She almost slipped until Stefan caught her hand in his and shielded her with his body. There was no end to the relentless questions, no lower depth that they could attribute to her motives.

Gritting her jaw, Clio followed Stefan's lead until one bold reporter shot out a hand and blocked Stefan's path.

"Give us one sentence, Mr. Bianco. Is Ms. Norwood just one of your usual arm candies or is there anything special about her?"

Stefan stilled and took in the crowd around them with a sly smile. Tugging her to his side, he wrapped an arm around her waist until she was plastered to him.

Something glittered in his gaze as he looked at her and a hundred flashes went on again to capture that mesmerizing look.

His gaze was molten fire, his mouth a study in sensuality.

Every inch of Clio gathered into a trembling ball at that heated look. He raised her hand to his face and kissed her knuckles, making sure the diamond on her finger caught the glare of every flash.

He played them so well.

Clio shivered uncontrollably. Gathering her against him, Stefan absorbed the tremors as if his solid, hard body was made for the very purpose of cushioning her and her emotions.

"After all these years, it didn't take us long to realize how perfect we are for each other. Ms. Norwood has done me the honor of agreeing to marry me, yes. And whoever else has been in her life until now, it's me she's walking to the altar with," he announced, possessiveness and pride dripping with each word, a flash of his Sicilian temperament wreathing his face.

It was all an act, Clio reminded herself, *a perfectly orchestrated one by a man who wanted to hit his opponent where it would hurt.*

The crowd went ballistic at the direct cut aimed toward Jackson. Her breath balling in her throat, she clung to Stefan's hard frame to stop from being mobbed with more questions.

She knew she should speak up, she knew that she was remaining calm just as she had done with Jackson. But for the life of her, she couldn't utter a word through the tightness in her chest.

She couldn't help but wish, with a powerless fury, that time would turn back.

Before Stefan had changed and before she had let herself be lost. Before life had woken them up to the gritty reality of it all.

"Mr. Bianco, will you settle down in New York now that your betrothed is here?"

"Will you make New York the base of operations for Bianco Luxury Real Estate?"

For the first time that evening, Clio saw a momentary doubt shadow Stefan's gaze.

His grip over her wrist tightened into a vise and she gasped.

Instantly, it loosened but he didn't break his stride to answer their questions this time.

Clio made it through most of the evening with herself intact. Of course, she had to remind herself more than a few times that what she and Stefan were putting on was an act.

Because it was intoxicating to be in the company of a man who didn't belittle anyone to prove his own worth, a man who could acknowledge the value of a competitor, a man whose confidence and self-belief was so bone deep that it was enthralling to watch for someone like her who had lost all sense of herself.

And because of their genuinely shared history, it was doubly easy to slip into the role of a loving fiancée, to finish each other's sentences, to laugh at a shared joke without having to communicate.

They fit together too well, as he had noted. More than one conservative businessman, some Stefan claimed had never liked him previously, dropped by to congratulate and backslap him.

To tell him in obvious terms that he had made a fantastic choice by finally giving up his playboy ways and turning into a family man.

His brows rose, he laughed as his cell phone continued to chime with calls from his board members from all over the globe.

The worst part of the evening was standing by him without betraying the shiver that went through her when he casually touched her every other minute.

A hand on her waist, a kiss on her cheek, the intimate way he pushed a strand of hair that had slipped from its knot behind her ear, the way his long fingers lingered over her nape, sometimes dipping lower, sometime pressing into the very spot on her shoulders where she was getting stiff.

The chemistry that they had discovered in Athens seemed only to grow exponentially even under the most innocent of touches.

It thrilled her and scared her equally.

Excusing herself, she made her way to the buffet table. Determined to look her best tonight, and at Stefan's urging, which was the nicest way to put his high-handed arranging of her day, Clio had spent most of the day lazing in the ultraluxurious spa at the Chatsfield, nibbling cucumber slices and drinking kale juice that had her looking supersuave in her designer dress—again arranged for her by her arrogant "fiancé"—but that had also left her on edge with hunger.

A migraine was looming, she was sure, and she wanted to stop it before it got worse.

She was about to grab a plate when her nape prickled, and a familiar scent sent her gut twisting into the most painful knot. She cast a look around and realized Jackson had her cornered.

"I didn't think you had it in you to lure someone of Bianco's stature. Fool me, huh, Clio?"

Nastiness dripped from every word Jackson uttered. But Clio held off the impulse to instantly scan the crowd for Stefan.

This had begun with Stefan at her side, true, but it was high time she looked after herself. Squaring her shoulders, she turned around.

His mouth curling, Jackson swept his blue gaze over her with such disdain that sweat pooled over her skin.

"Don't make a scene, Jackson."

"Oh, come on, Clio. After that entrance, after that clip of you crawling all over him out there for the world to see… after you jumped into his bed without even telling me we're through, you disgust me."

That he could think all that of her, that he could say it to her face stunned Clio.

"You're the one who's been fooling me for months," she said, unable to curb the words from falling out of her mouth. All the warnings she had given herself about not betraying what she had seen flew out. Her throat felt like there was glass stuck in it and she had to remind herself that it was not her shame.

"God, you had sex with Ashley and you laughed at me with her."

Something like shame filled his gaze, and was gone in a nanosecond, a calculating look emerging in his features. "So that's what this is about? Payback? You think you'll dangle yourself on his arm and make me sorry for what I did? You think I'll come running back to you and beg for forgiveness?"

His gaze took in her designer dress, her upswept hair, the diamond on her finger as if he was cataloging everything about her.

Venomous satisfaction filled his gaze. "Of course it is. Why else would a red-blooded Sicilian like *Bianco*, who's known to never date a woman for more than a week, want to marry you of all the women on the planet?"

For the first time since she had heard the sound of him shamelessly shagging his assistant, Clio was filled with molten fury unlike she had ever known.

It was cleansing, it was invigorating and it burned any remaining doubt that somehow, it had been her fault.

She had done nothing wrong except for trusting a deceptive man with not an ounce of honor.

"You have pushed me beyond my limits already but be careful what you say about him. Stefan already doesn't have much of an opinion about you."

"You stupid whore," he spat out, fear and something else shaking his well-muscled frame. "Can't you see he's just using you to get to me?"

They were drawing looks, she was aware of it as if there was another version of her scanning the room. Years of breeding and her own nature cringed at being amidst a spectacle, recoiled at being the center of attention. But she was damned if she let Jackson intimidate her, too, on top of everything else he had done.

"Don't you dare take another step forward, Jackson."

Something in her tone must have registered because he stopped, his mouth still wearing that nasty curl. "The minute he realizes you're of no use to him, just as you weren't to me, he's going to dump your ass.

"He's no more going to marry you than I did in three years. And when he does dump you, when he moves on to brighter and better pastures, I'll still be here to laugh at you, Clio.

"You're nothing but a crutch to be used."

The knowing smile on his lips, the sneering tone of his words, the decided gleam in his eyes that there was nothing valuable about her to any man, the echo of her darkest fear that no man would ever love her for herself and not her name—it unleashed a firestorm in Clio.

She wanted to roar at Jackson, she wanted to raise her hand and slap the sneer off his mouth.

But he didn't even deserve her anger.

Lifting her head high, she gave him an imperious look that cut him to size. "Be prepared to lose, Jackson. Everything," she said loudly, glad that she sounded steady, confident.

She could not let him ruin what was left of her life in the city that she loved so much. She would not let him run her out of New York on a wave of scandal and shame. She could not let him still have so much power over her life, her happiness.

Even if it meant taking the biggest gamble she had ever risked in her life, even if it meant tying her fate to the one man who could help her become whole again, even if he did it by shredding her to pieces.

"You'll be glad that you're the first one to hear this. Stefan and I are going to be married in a week. Here in New York, at the Chatsfield. And you know what, Jackson? You're invited."

Dio, no!

Clio hadn't just said that.

Standing at the back of the crowd that was hungrily lapping up the exchange between Clio and that scum, Jackson, Stefan stood rooted to the spot, a hundred different emotions crashing and derailing him from inside.

It felt eerily like that moment when Serena had callously and without even an ounce of emotion told him that she was done with him, that she had no use for him without his parents' fortune.

In just a minute, he had lost everything—his parents' respect and trust and love, the woman he had given up everything for, and the worst, his belief in his judgment, his emotions, in his self-worth.

His entire world had collapsed.

Her shoulders ramrod straight, her eyes breathing green fire, her small breasts falling and rising, her skin glowing with anger—it was the Clio he had admired and lusted after a decade ago.

She was spectacular to behold, truly an equal to goddess Athena at that moment as she battled the obvious fear that shadowed her gaze.

But even above the fierce pride and admiration he felt on her behalf for finally putting Jackson in his place was the most insidiously ugly and eviscerating thought he had ever faced.

Her boldness in so publicly and irrevocably announcing their wedding in a week…

Had this been her plan all along? Had the distrust and fragility in her eyes, the way she had trembled under his lips, the shadow of the woman that made him want to protect her from everything, had it all been an act?

The minute the thought erupted, Stefan felt acidic distaste flood his mouth. Cursing, he drove his fist into the pillar next to him, attempting to ground himself, struggling to contain his volatile emotions and his mind's poisonous thoughts.

Dio, he didn't want to think along either lines about Clio. And yet the distrust in him was bone deep.

Even as he hated that she was changing his life, even as he couldn't get a handle on his suspicions, he knew how much making a life here meant to her, knew how much she loved this city.

Reminded himself of the desperate courage that had shone in her eyes when she had shown up at his suite.

Running a hand along his brow, he looked back at her.

Jackson was nowhere to be seen and she was surrounded by well-wishers.

A little of the color was back in her cheeks as her gaze swept through the hall, looking for him.

She had more than surprised him, true. But she couldn't

be allowed to indulge in it again, couldn't be allowed to warrant this much emotion from him—whether surprise or fury or this want for her that was becoming a force he couldn't fight.

If she wanted him to marry her, there was only one way that he could do it.

CHAPTER SEVEN

WHEN CLIO HAD moved a decade ago to study at Columbia, New York, the young, handsome playboys she had become friends with had captivated her. Even through the hardest times over the past decade, she had never once considered returning home to England. She had had such spectacular plans for when she would marry, where she would live for the rest of her life.

But she had never meant to make her dream come true this way. Catching back the sigh that wanted to escape, she looked up at Stefan, streetlights and huge ads bathing his face in strips of light.

The hardest New York winter held less frost than Stefan's gaze in the interior of the limo. For the rest of the evening and the drive back to Manhattan, they hadn't exchanged a single word.

Gazing out through the windows, he kept his phone glued to his ear the entire length of the drive. And judging from his conversation, Clio realized he was handling a crisis with his holdings in Asia.

It was a small comfort that he wasn't freezing her out intentionally as she waited on tenterhooks for his reaction.

If he had snarled at her, if he had called her a hundred names, if he had let that fiery temper explode and lashed out at her, Clio would have had some estimate of his reaction.

But this silent chill that he seemed to radiate from every pore, for the first time since she had seen him standing on the terrace of the Empire State Building, arrogance and power emanating from him, left Clio afraid.

Even the ruthless stranger she had come to know this past week would have been welcome.

Feeling a lead weight in her chest, Clio followed him through the gleaming entryway into the soaring luxury hotel steeped in tradition. Every inch of the plush interior screamed over-the-top opulence and extravagance.

Nothing but the best for Stefan Bianco.

But every time she walked in through the doors of the Chatsfield, saw the eager staff greet Stefan, Clio was reminded of the fact that Stefan didn't own a home. Anywhere in the world. He lived aboard his private jet, flying across the globe as his business dictated, without any connection to the world.

And here in New York, of all places, he hadn't even intended to stay past the week.

They had decided they would just leave it as an open-ended engagement. Scary prospect as it had been, she had even started looking for a new job.

The walls felt like they would cave in on them and trap them in the tension forever as the steel doors of the elevator closed and they were carried to the penthouse suite.

The unobstructed panoramic views of Manhattan from the suite's glass balconies didn't fascinate her as they usually did. The glittering diamond skylights, the floor-to-ceiling windows, the unique artwork alongside stunning artifacts... nothing held her interest tonight.

It was the silent man who did.

Without taking his gaze off of her, he undid his cuffs. Next came the buttons on his dress shirt. Clio held his gaze, even as the shadow of his olive skin under the shirt beckoned.

The column of his throat was a visual feast as were the chiseled angles of his face.

"Damn it, Stefan. Say something."

ing but a carefully constructed projection
r eyes, until there was nothing but empti-
..

who he was, no woman was herself with

uldn't hesitate to be herself with him was
unlike anything. It morphed his physical
nto something else…

ondered about that even temper of yours,
year at Columbia I would spend hours won-
er lost it and how you would look if you did,"
d tugged at her hair.

us hair tumbled down to her shoulders like
ll holding her with one hand, he twisted the
s fingers. Wondered for the millionth time
d look wearing nothing.

in my life even hurt a fly," she muttered, but
asky and uneven.

tic satisfaction filled him. She was just as
he was, struggling with her want even as she
for doubting her.

kes me feel extra special."

ecause you're an utter bastard."

're learning, Clio."

his face in her hair and breathed deeply.

s a freedom that she understood him now. That
lly learned he was not the friend she remem-
uch fondness. That the man he was now could
motives and yet still want her with a feral need
o reason.

realized he was not doing this for her but be-
desperate need to bring down Jackson.

d not trust him now, would not expect anything
nd there was a relief in it.

, she sagged against him, as if the fight depleted
nd he relaxed his arms around her.

Not even Jackson's ugly name-calling shredded her composure as Stefan's silence did.

His olive green gaze was hard, flinty even. "I have never been maneuvered into a corner so publicly and so irrevocably, *bella*. I think I have been rendered mute."

Maneuvered? Her stomach tying in knots, Clio blinked. There was no anger in his words, no resentment in his tone. Something else lingered there on a razor's edge, waiting to strike.

"Stefan, I don't know what came over me. I have never lost my temper like that."

His posture screamed careless lounging but Clio knew he noticed every breath she took, every nuance that crossed her face.

"I know it's not something you ask a friend over dinner, but I would owe you…" Shaking her head, Clio caught the words in her mouth. In her wildest dreams, she had never thought she would beg a man to marry her, to ask someone to turn such a big lie into reality.

She reconsidered it in her own head.

If she didn't value herself, no one else would. Not Jackson, not the world and definitely not Stefan.

And she needed Stefan to value her, to respect her. Suddenly, it felt like the most important thing in the world that he did, that she become at least half the person he had known a decade ago.

"I'll bring you everything I can on him, Stefan. This is my city, and my life. I will not let him steal any more from me."

"Think carefully, Clio. You might only be exchanging one awful man for another. Because I'll not change anything in my life for a woman, *cara*. Not even a surprise wife."

Now there was no taunting smile, there was no lazy charm, only utter seriousness in his gaze. Urgency pounding through her, she reached him and grabbed the lapels of his shirt. Thrust her face so close to his that the masculine heat of him swathed her, pinging across her skin, infiltrating every cell and pore. "What do you mean?"

The rhythmic whir of the fax machine in the open study as it cranked out documents filled the cavernous lounge. The sound chafed against her skin as Clio waited for an answer, her breath suspended in her throat.

Grasping her wrists, he pushed her back. Prowled to the fax machine and returned with a sheaf of papers.

He produced a gold-tipped fountain pen from somewhere and nodded toward the sheaf of papers.

"It means the marriage will be only in name, *Clio*, a contractual agreement that we will both sign. It means all you will get from me is a peanut allowance. It means you'll sign a prenuptial contract and a nondisclosure agreement that you won't reveal any of this to another soul or sell the story or write a *memoir* of our life together at a later time.

"It means you won't dictate who occupies my bed after we're both through with Jackson, and you'll not throw allegations of love at me.

"If you accept and then violate any of the above, the consequences will be far-reaching."

Clio gasped for breath, as if someone had kicked her in the gut, as if something icy and vicious had been stuck in her chest. Tears pricked behind her eyelids, her lungs struggling to breathe.

"You think…*you actually think* I planned all this?" she poked him in the chest, hurt splintering into a millions shards. "You think I orchestrated it so that our farcical engagement turns into a real marriage and I can mooch off your millions?"

"The thought crossed my mind, *sì*," he said, without blinking, without a beat, without wondering how much pain he was causing her with his casually elegant shrug.

Clio slapped him so hard that her arm jerked at the impact. Her entire body shuddered but it was still nothing compared to the sharp pain in her chest.

Before she could
against his hard body
grip, her breasts crus
with the scent of him.

Stefan didn't know wl
Clio had actually slap
to it.

He had to have truly
the sight of her—out of
ruffled, her composure
turned him on as if a fire

That he had driven he
a win more than anything

He turned rock hard an

He held her hands tight
her breasts rubbed agains
nipples visible against the
gaze. The scent of her perfu

Dio, the woman smelled

He moved his free hand
over hers. She was so silky so
dered to other areas. "Corne
slap me second…no woman
you have achieved today, *tes*

She pushed at him again
budged at her attack. "Don't
ever the hell it means."

"Then do not push me in
know, *bella*."

The more she struggled ag
he became. He gave himself
joyed the novelty of his own n

Most of the women he had
been simpering, talking him u
before he even knew it. Until o

until he was no
of himself in th
ness inside him
No one knev
him…
That Clio w
an aphrodisia
hunger for her
"I always v
bella. That firs
dering if you e
he drawled, a
Her gorge
amber fire. S
hair around l
how she wou
"I've neve
it came out l
An atavi
turned on as
despised hir
"That ma
"That's b
"Now yo
He burie
There wa
she had fina
bered with s
distrust her
that knew n
That she
cause of his
She wou
from him a
Suddenly
out of her.

"Why are you doing this?" she finally said in such a small voice that it shook him more than her slap had.

"Because it's impossible for me to trust your motive, unbearable for me to give a woman place in my life, even temporarily. Isn't that clear enough, *bella*? The fact that I'm even contemplating doing this is because I need that proof, Clio. But make sure you don't up the price any more.

"If you accept, we'll be married next week. Here at the Chatsfield, just as you want. We will show Jackson and New York a wedding they won't forget soon. You'll be the most beautiful bride New York has ever seen."

A shiver racked Clio and instantly his hold on her tightened, his body a deceptively warm fortress around her.

"I will sign wherever you want me to, I will follow every condition of yours. I have…*lost* so much already, I… You'll have your revenge," she said bitterly. "There's definitely something fishy with Jackson's numbers."

"Good," he replied, stepping away from her.

He had shown her his true self and yet, it felt as if he was the one who had been burned.

"Good night, Stefan," Clio whispered, her throat aching, her gut churning in panic.

What had she done? Oh, God, what had she done? How could she have not seen what her enraged, impulsive declaration would turn him into?

Without casting another glance at him, she walked away, her head held high.

For the first time in a decade, Stefan felt the landscape of his life slip from his fingers and all because of a woman. Again.

The only way he knew to protect Clio and himself from this was to set rules, to remove her from his mind, to wipe and forget the taste of her from his thoughts and definitely decouple her from his lust.

To set expectations that neither of them could falter over.

Crushing the overwhelming urge to kiss the hurt away from her mouth, he walked into his office and turned on the huge plasma screens mounted over the far wall.

Walking into the closet, he stripped and dressed in his workout shorts. Cranked up the rowing machine he'd had specially installed in his study and went to work on it.

He was not only seething against the course he had set tonight, but he had sexual frustration added to the mix.

Just the cranking of the machine and the burn of his thigh and arm muscles went a long way toward calming him down.

The news would already be spreading, he knew.

The fact that he—the quintessential third bachelor among the Columbia Four—was finally getting married, and in just a week, so soon after Rocco's and Christian's fairy-tale weddings, would unleash a storm he couldn't contain.

A picture of him and Clio entering the Chatsfield tonight, immediately followed by a shot of them from a decade ago, lounging on the steps of University Hall at Columbia with wide smiles on their faces, flashed on the screen.

Not everyone trusts a corporation with a predatory play-boy at its helm, he had heard his board bemoan more than once when he had questioned why they hadn't made a particular deal.

An evening of being an affianced man—and to Clio—had already changed the business world's perception of him. And stealing Clio from Jackson, as the media was calling it, meant that the focus stayed on his business and him.

It worked for his business and his brand to have a wife, and Clio at that, who was sophisticated and levelheaded and, more important, had no expectations of him. Even if she had, he had made sure he had destroyed them tonight.

It worked every which way he looked at it except for his heart.

Hearing the phrase "Reunited College Sweethearts" stuck in his craw. He was the last man who should have a *fairy-tale love story come true* line attached to his name. He was the last man Clio should have come to for help, he acknowledged now with bitter resignation.

Because, even if he wanted to, he couldn't change himself now. The poison Serena had brought into his life had infused his very blood.

All he cared about now was destroying Jackson and keeping himself and Clio intact until the end of this marriage.

"If you want to leave all this behind, *leave Stefan behind,*" Zayed whispered in her ear even as he amiably tucked her bare arm along his under the watchful, hawk-like gaze of Stefan at the end of the vast hall on the other side, "then all you have to do is say so, Clio. I shall signal Rocco and a limousine will appear outside the hotel in a matter of seconds. In a few hours, you can be in Milan, or Hong Kong, or even Gazbiyaa if you don't mind the stark and beautiful desert land of a country on the brink of war."

Blinking, Clio tore her gaze away from Stefan's olive green one. The Chatsfield glittered, and the hungry hush of designer-clad guests, a power list of New York's Who's Who, reached her in stifling waves.

They were all here to witness her union with one of the most sought-after bachelors in the world. Reminding herself to smile like a woman madly in love, she pasted a smile and turned toward Zayed.

And caught the scowl on her fiancé's face in the infinitesimal moment before she turned.

They were standing at the entrance to the Terrace Room, as it was called, just beyond the French doors of the courtyard of the Chatsfield, a room steeped in history and charm.

The room boasted some of the most impressive historical detailing, created in the spirit of the Italian Renaissance. Exquisite crystal chandeliers hung from the ceiling, bathing the vast room in a golden glow.

Swallowing at the hard knot in her throat, she clutched

Zayed's fingers tightly and he returned the pressure. "I thought your loyalty would be to Stefan, Your Highness."

"Not you, too, Clio," Zayed warned her, still a glimmer of the playboy prince in his smile. In just a matter of days, Zayed had gone from second son to the ruler of Gazbiyaa. And Clio couldn't even begin to imagine what must be going on in his head.

"I thought you would warn Stefan away from me, not the opposite."

His deep brown eyes shining with kindness, his mouth set into that diplomatic half smile, Zayed shook his head. Why hadn't she gone to him for help instead of the stubborn Sicilian?

"You forget that Rocco, Christian and I know you as well as Stefan does. And Stefan…he is more than a brother to me, but we have seen him become jaded and more hardened than the rest of us. I wouldn't want my enemy's daughter to be caught in that disdain of his. And *you*…you're a friend, Clio."

Clio hugged the warmth in his tone. "He did not force me into anything, Zayed," she said, wanting to make sure they all understood. Every step of the way, Stefan had only prepared her for what was coming, including his disdain.

"This was my choice." Whether right or wrong, she was glad that it was.

Zayed's expression didn't waver. "None of us want you to be hurt, Clio. He could very possibly do it, and then he won't forgive himself, no?"

Her gut sinking, Clio finally understood their concern, understood the friction she had sensed between Stefan and the three of them the past two days.

Stefan thought they were all protecting her from him.

What he didn't realize was that Rocco, Christian and Zayed were also looking out for him. They were afraid that by hurting her, he was going to irrevocably lose a part of himself.

A tightness emerged in her chest at the very thought and the sinking realization of how complicated the man she was about to marry was.

It's the only way I can do this, Clio, he had said to her when she had signed the contract.

Was it the only way he thought of to protect their fragile relationship from what they were putting it through? And she resolved to not lose him, not to let this mutual need for revenge destroy them.

"I won't let that happen, Zayed."

Whether he believed her or not, Zayed patted her hand. "You have friends, Clio. Always remember that."

Wetness filled her eyes, but Clio smiled through it.

Rocco and Olivia, Christian and Alessandra, and Zayed—all of them had hovered over her the past few days like mother hens.

It had felt incredibly good to know she had so many people who cared about her well-being.

With every detail of the most opulent wedding she had ever dreamed of taken care of, with the grand hotel decorated ornately for what the media were calling the "Fairy-Tale Wedding of the Decade," with people who actually cared about her surrounding her, for a few compelling moments over the past week she could have almost fooled herself into believing it was the wedding she had wanted all her life.

Except for the man in the center of it all who hadn't even looked her in the eye in a week, who had only spoken to her to discuss another blasted clause in the contract he had made her sign.

He had engaged an army of people to oversee every small detail of the wedding. Clio had barely had time to have second thoughts about how big a step she was taking.

Designers and lawyers, makeup artists and wedding planners—there hadn't been a single thing that Clio herself had been responsible for. All she had to do was nod, and maybe use her brain cells to make a choice as to whether she wanted lilies or orchids or another exotic flower she couldn't even remember the name of, whether she wanted chocolate cake or red velvet.

She had blanched when she had discreetly looked up the designer who had been hired to create her wedding gown in a week.

With delicate corded lace on tulle skimming the shoulders and neckline, the fragile gown had a line of buttons sneaking downward between her shoulder blades.

It was the most beautiful dress she had ever seen, and she couldn't swallow the fact that it had been created with her in mind. Diamond bracelets, befitting Stefan Bianco's intended, she had been told when she had argued, had been delivered in a velvet box, along with matching diamond earrings and the most elegantly designed diamond tiara.

She had been stunned at her own reflection, at how perfect the dress was for her slim build, how well it accentuated her almost boyish curves.

The diamonds had glittered and winked in the three full-length mirrors the hotel staff had set up.

And that's when it had hit her.

The money he was spending on the wedding—she had given up adding once she had looked through the hotel's website.

Which meant the cost of the wedding had to be astronomical.

Feeling as dirty as Jackson had called her, she had knocked on his study door one evening.

To find him at the rowing machine, dressed in shorts and bathed in sweat. It was a sight that was burned into her brain, her skin, her very cells.

The sight of his curling biceps, ropes of sweat-slicked muscles in his chest and back, the sleek contours of his torso, dissolved every brain cell into mush.

God, they had been rowing champions at Columbia, the

YOUR PARTICIPATION IS REQUESTED!

Dear Reader,

Since you are a lover of our books – we would like to get to know you!

Inside you will find a short Reader's Survey. Sharing your answers with us will help our editorial staff understand who you are and what activities you enjoy.

To thank you for your participation, we would like to send you 2 books and 2 gifts – **ABSOLUTELY FREE!**

Enjoy your gifts with our appreciation,

Pam Powers

**SEE INSIDE
FOR READER'S
SURVEY**

For Your Reading Pleasure...

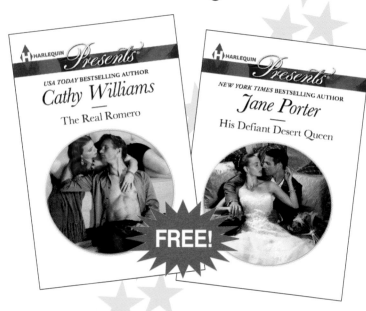

We'll send you 2 books and 2 gifts
ABSOLUTELY FREE
just for completing our Reader's Survey!

YOUR READER'S SURVEY
"THANK YOU" FREE GIFTS INCLUDE:
- ▶ **2 FREE books**
- ▶ **2 lovely surprise gifts**

▶ DETACH AND MAIL CARD TODAY! ▶

PLEASE **FILL** IN THE CIRCLES COMPLETELY TO RESPOND

1) What type of fiction books do you enjoy reading? (Check all that apply)
- ○ Suspense/Thrillers   ○ Action/Adventure   ○ Modern-day Romances
- ○ Historical Romance   ○ Humour   ○ Paranormal Romance

2) What attracted you most to the last fiction book you purchased on impulse?
- ○ The Title   ○ The Cover   ○ The Author   ○ The Story

3) What is usually the greatest influencer when you <u>plan</u> to buy a book?
- ○ Advertising   ○ Referral   ○ Book Review

4) How often do you access the internet?
- ○ Daily ○ Weekly ○ Monthly ○ Rarely or never.

5) How many NEW paperback fiction novels have you purchased in the past 3 months?
- ○ 0 - 2   ○ 3 - 6   ○ 7 or more

YES! I have completed the Reader's Survey. Please send me the 2 FREE books and 2 FREE gifts (gifts are worth about $10) for which I qualify. I understand that I am under no obligation to purchase any books, as explained on the back of this card.

❏ I prefer the regular-print edition
106/306 HDL GH5M

❏ I prefer the larger-print edition
176/376 HDL GH5M

FIRST NAME	LAST NAME

ADDRESS

APT.#	CITY

STATE/PROV.	ZIP/POSTAL CODE

four of them. And he still looked just as fit as he had been a decade ago, if not better. She had spent several minutes staring at him, heat uncoiling in her lower belly, every inch of her body vibrating with desire.

When she had finally found her voice and expressed her concerns, he had cast her a look that was like a bucket of ice-cold water over her heated senses.

"Don't worry, *bella*," he had said, rising to his feet. His thick hair was curled with sweat. "This doesn't count against you. After all, our whole agreement rests on the pretense that I want to throw the love of my life the wedding of her dreams, *sì*?"

Faced with that mocking scorn, Clio had had to fight against the instinct to rush out of there. "I have been going over the seating charts and I didn't see your parents' names," she finally managed.

His expression shut down instantly, as if a light had gone out. "They're not coming."

A warning vibrated in his answer. But instead of heeding it, her mind thought back to them. The rest of the Columbia Four and her included, had all envied Stefan his parents' unconditional love more than anything.

The Biancos were those picture-perfect Sicilian parents for whom family came first and foremost always. And it had been a shock when they had threatened to cut him off if he didn't come back home after graduation.

And Stefan hadn't cared about his inheritance. Only Serena had betrayed him when she realized he wouldn't have the Bianco fortune behind him.

"Stefan, your parents…they forgave you, didn't they? For trusting Serena?"

"I have not asked them for it, *bella*."

Why? "Wait, you haven't… I don't understand."

His gaze unblinking, he opened the door for her, his withdrawal sending the room into subzero temperatures. "They are not on the guest list because I didn't invite them, *cara*. We don't need to involve any more people in our deception, do we?"

"No," Clio had replied, reeling from the frost in his words.

What had he meant by that? Had he not seen his parents all these years? How could he bear to keep them at a distance like that?

In that moment, Clio had realized what an utter stranger he was to her.

His distrust of her motives, his insistence that they do it per his rules, the cold front he presented if she asked anything personal—she finally understood he wasn't just lost to her.

He *had* buried everything good and decent about him. But before she left his life, before he was through with her, she was determined to remind him what he had been once. And she had to begin with bringing his parents back into his life.

Hers would never forgive her, but Stefan...he could have his parents back.

"Clio?"

Coloring, Clio looked at Zayed. "Thank you so much for reminding me that I have friends, Zayed." She blew a long breath out, remembering her mother's unforgiving words, and their blatant refusal to come. Reminded herself that she had friends who would always stick by her. "And for agreeing to give me away."

"You did me an honor when you asked me." Still smiling, he cast a quick look ahead. "I can feel Stefan's gaze drilling holes in my head. Not even my enemy country's politics make me shudder so," he said with a mock shiver. "Are you ready for him, Clio?"

Sucking in a deep breath, Clio turned toward her waiting bridegroom.

Dressed in a black evening suit, his thick hair combed back, he stood out so prominently amidst the rest of the men.

He had promised her he would help her. And that he kept his word—even though a wedding, even of the fake kind, clearly filled him with utter fury—she hugged it to herself.

Whatever else he claimed, Stefan Bianco was a man of honor.

"I'm ready, Zayed," she whispered.

Her hold on the lilies in her hand shaky, she followed Zayed's lead as the music began.

With both her parents and Stefan's not in attendance, she had decided to do without a maid of honor, electing to stick to the traditions only by a bit. Somehow it felt as if it fit them—this wedding among friends who were their true family, in the city that had welcomed them with open arms a decade ago.

Everything about the wedding was perfection itself. Even the weather was a beautiful June day, gorgeous with the sun shining.

It wasn't a real marriage, Clio reminded herself as they reached Stefan and Zayed handed her over. It was all a story they were creating for the media and Jackson.

Her heart zigzagged all over the place as Stefan clasped her fingers tight in his.

But as she met his gaze for the first time in a week and saw the dark, possessive fire flickering to life there, she shivered.

How was she supposed to resist him when the liquid lust in his eyes felt like the only real thing today? How was she supposed to resist him when despite his distrust of her, he made her feel as if she mattered?

CHAPTER EIGHT

HE HAD A WIFE.

One who was dressed in delicate white lace that displayed her alabaster skin in its glory. The row of buttons going all the way to her lower back was all he could think of.

Her flaming hair, combed back into a tight knot at the back, the long line of her jaw and neck were a temptation for his fingers.

Her dress, while lacy, was elegant, sophisticated, as it hugged her lithe frame and small breasts.

She looked as she always did—demure, stylish, perfectly put together. Only he knew what simmered beneath that calm exterior.

He had a wife and he couldn't turn his gaze away from her.

The thought was so disconcerting and disturbing that Stefan kept turning the platinum band on his finger round and round, as if he could make it disappear, as if he could change reality by stubbornly refusing to accept it.

He not only had a wife but one he wanted to kiss more than he needed to drag in his next breath.

And the most shocking fact of them all was that his new wife had almost flinched when he had touched her lips with his.

He, Stefan Bianco, the man who had dated some of the most beautiful, accomplished women in the world, badly wanted to touch and kiss and seduce his wife, the one woman he should never touch or want in any way.

It was how he had felt when he had first eyed Clio across the campus lawn a decade ago—full of raging hormones, and an almost laughable naïveté about the world.

He still wanted her just as badly except now that naïveté was dead and in its place was a voice that kept whispering that he could have Clio if he wanted this time.

Like the rest of the women in the world, Clio Norwood had a price, too. And he had already paid the price.

It was such a disgusting line of thought that nausea filled his throat. And yet he couldn't erase it.

Was this what he had become? Was there nothing honorable left in him?

For the first time in years, Stefan looked inward and cringed, wondered what else he had lost in the name of Serena.

"You'll break the champagne flute if you don't stop glaring at Zayed and Clio, *fratello*," Rocco whispered from behind him.

He couldn't blame his oldest friend for the continual jeering because what Stefan wanted to do was throw the champagne flute on the dance floor so that Clio would stop smiling at Zayed and look back at him.

"She's always been a beautiful dancer, hasn't she?" Christian chimed in, and now the vein in Stefan's temple felt as if it would burst open.

He knew very well what his three friends were up to. He also knew very well that Rocco had eyes for no one but Olivia, and Christian for his pregnant wife, the beautiful Alessandra.

In the rational part of his mind, the increasingly small one, he was also aware that as much as Zayed seemed to be whispering little jokes in Clio's ear and had been flirting with her outrageously for most of the evening, he had never had any interest in Clio.

Even if he hadn't guessed that the fairy tale that Clio and he were projecting to the whole world was just that—a tale of epic proportions.

But knowing it and telling his body and his libido to behave accordingly was another thing.

Because the moment he had slid the gold band onto her trembling finger, the moment he had touched her lips with his own, the moment he saw the despondency in her eyes as she slid the ring onto his finger, Stefan had felt the most possessive, an almost Neanderthal, urge to drag Clio away from the celebration that followed and ravish her.

He wanted to drive the thought of another man from her mind, he wanted to kiss away the hurt from her mouth, he wanted to shred her control as she was so effortlessly shredding his.

He wanted her to smile at him as she did at the whole world, even though he had done everything to wipe it from her face.

He wanted to sink into her wet heat again and again, until the small fancy, which was now growing into a full-blown obsession, was gone from his blood.

He could seduce her, too. He had no doubt about it. Whatever poison that asshole Jackson had spewed into her mind, whatever she believed about her own nature—because there had been plenty of occasions over the past week to figure it out—there was an explosive energy every time they occupied the same space.

Something his all-too-clever and observant friends had remarked over the past week. But if there was one thing Stefan didn't want, it was to see that betrayal in Clio's eyes the next morning. She would never sleep with him and then walk away unscathed. And as fragile as she was right now, he didn't want to be another bad decision she regretted.

He wanted her to be consumed by him as he was by her. Which seemed a far-out fantasy right then.

If he could forget the contract they had signed, he could have almost believed her to be the old Clio, having the time of her life, supremely happy with her life and the world.

Except when she looked at him. Then, the smile fell off her face as if she had eaten something that lived under those gold-lined slippers she was wearing.

Except when it had been their dance. She had been stiff like a board, her features frozen into a mask of icy politeness, so tightly withdrawn that he could break her with a hard grip.

She had hardly touched her dinner but her face had lit up when it had been time for the red-velvet cake they had cut together.

Every time she had lifted the gleaming spoon and licked away the dessert, Stefan smothered a groan himself.

"Come have a drink with us," said Rocco, interrupting Stefan's thoughts as they veered into dangerous territory about how snugly Zayed was holding Clio and how neatly she fit against his tall, wide frame. Tendrils of hair were beginning to come away from her elaborate hairstyle and kiss that delicate jawline.

He heard another laugh fall from those beautiful lips, saw her tilt her head and whisper something and he'd had enough.

He was on the dance floor and cutting in on Zayed and Clio before he knew what he was doing. As though guessing that he was as rational as a charging bull, his friend instantly relinquished Clio, a cunning smile in his eyes.

Among the four of them, Zayed was the diplomat, yet Stefan didn't doubt for a second that he was also the most perceptive. With a slap on his back, Zayed pulled him closer into a hug.

There was no humor in his gaze just then. "Take care, Stefan. Our fate cannot always be controlled by us, my friend."

Stefan didn't smile either. He knew he had become an untenable, mistrusting bastard in the past few years, that he had pushed Rocco to the limit by doubting the wonderful Olivia's intentions toward his friend, but Rocco, Christian and Zayed—they had always stood by him and loved him no matter what.

That was the only relationship, the one good thing Serena hadn't destroyed in his life, an anchor that had held him steady when he had been sinking.

"You think I'm capable of falling in love, Zayed?"

"No, I do not. I don't think you or I will have the fortune that has been bestowed on Rocco and Christian, nor do we want it. But do not destroy the good that has somehow found its way into your life."

With Zayed's advice ringing in his ears, Stefan tugged his new bride toward him. Every muscle in his body tensed when she came into his arms pliantly, wrapped her arms around his neck.

Her small breasts rubbed against his chest, one toned thigh pressing flush against his muscular one. She smelled decadent, her skin soft like the sheerest silk. His pulse thudded heavily in his blood, the delicate crook of her neck and shoulders beckoning for a taste.

Wrapping his fingers around her nape, Stefan tugged her head back and looked into her eyes and received another shock.

"You...need to lighten up, my dear husband," she whispered against his cheek, dragging her mouth over his stubble, toward his jaw. "We're supposed to be madly in love, remember?"

Her touch was possessive, reckless, and it made him want it everywhere, made him forget right and wrong.

Clasping her cheeks, he pushed her chin up to meet his eyes.

His new wife was utterly sloshed.

Something akin to a burn began in his chest as he looked into her eyes, the blacks dilated against the glittering green. Tucking loose tendrils of her hair beneath her ear, Stefan picked her up to rising cheers and comments from the guests.

Clio had never imagined that she would be drunk on her wedding night. She had never thought she would feel like a half terrified, half hopeful Victorian virgin that the pirate would carry aboard his ship and ravish.

In the past couple of years when Jackson had evaded all talk of their wedding with such skilled precision, she hadn't imagined she would ever have a wedding, much less a wedding night.

So with everything that had gone sideways in her life, the fact that she was drunk was the least disconcerting thing about the night.

Not that she had planned it that way.

She had signed the agreement as he wanted her to. She had smiled and gushed like a woman in love so much that her jaw had begun to hurt. She had tried not to flinch and betray the trembling need she felt when he touched his soft, hot mouth to hers.

Not once during the day had she behaved in a wifely manner whatsoever.

So she had no idea what it was that had turned Stefan more and more distant and forbidding. Unless, it was the very sight of her wearing his ring.

With him radiating an icy scorn from every pore at her side wherever she turned or whoever she looked at all evening, she had drunk her first glass of champagne without getting any food first.

Of course, she had devoured her cake—which sadly was the high point of her wedding day, but by then she had already had a buzz. Which made it all too easy to reach for the second one.

It had made her unafraid, as she had been a long time ago. *Unafraid, uncaring and free.*

And because she had loved being that old Clio again, even if it was the alcohol, she had drunk two more glasses. Even the thought of a head-splitting migraine that was sure to arrive first thing tomorrow hadn't stopped her.

She had thoroughly enjoyed dancing with Rocco and Christian, and Zayed flirting with her. He had done it out of pity because her very real husband couldn't even fake a smile, much less pretend to be besotted. Still, she had enjoyed it.

The most disturbing thing about the night, however, was the solid hard muscular chest that she was cradled against with utmost care right now. The scent of his aftershave— lime—teased her nostrils.

But she didn't want to be held like that, she didn't want him to suffer her company as if he was cursed to do it.

Just then, the elevator rocked.

Giving up any effort at a pretense, Clio sighed and clutched him tighter.

Then she felt it more than heard it—the choked-up, almost suppressed laugh that had his chest rumbling beneath her arms. Cracking her eyes open, Clio dared a look at him.

He was laughing.

The beast who had glared at her all evening, who had looked at her as if she was the most untrustworthy woman on the entire planet, no the universe, who had driven her to drink when she generally couldn't stand alcohol, was laughing.

Granted, to see that sensuous, cutting-grooves-in-his-cheeks smile was *almost* worth any price.

Thrusting her hands under the collar of his dress shirt, Clio tucked his chin up until he was staring into her eyes. "What the hell are you laughing about?"

"You, *bella*," he replied.

"What about me?"

"A Victorian virgin aboard a pirate ship that was about to be ravished?"

Heat swarmed her face. God, she had said that out loud?

"I'm drunk," she drawled, loving the *thump-thump* of his heart beneath her ears. He was so solid and warm around her that perversely, she felt safe around him. "Anything I say tonight should be disregarded," she retorted. "And I'm no Victorian virgin that needs to be ravished or for that matter saved."

"Seeing that I'm not the saving-hero kind, that's good." The elevator doors swished open. And he stepped out. "It's almost scary how perfect we are for each other."

"'College Sweethearts Who Found Their Way to Each Other After So Many Years'?" she said, quoting the headlines about them. "'Destiny Brings Old Lovers Together Again!' 'True Love Conquers All.' I wouldn't have wanted a better tagline for Jackson to look at every time he turned his head."

Instantly, the smile slid off his mouth as if she had poisoned the very air around them. There was such a bright ire in his gaze that Clio wondered for a second if he would let her fall to the floor.

But, of course, he didn't.

Stefan would never cause her harm, she knew that. Just as he would never trust her any more than a strange woman he picked up in a club or a party or wherever he picked up women from.

She had thought she had accepted it, but it was beginning to matter more than it should. Even if she had fallen on her face these past few years, didn't he know what kind of a person she was?

He crossed the cavernous lounge and carried her into one of the bedrooms at the back.

He slowly brought her to her feet. Miscalculating the buzz in her head, she swayed and he caught her.

His arms came around her from behind to steady her.

Her body operating on its own, Clio sagged against him. But his arms were like iron vises around her waist, holding her still, stopping her from leaning back.

A devil inside goading her, Clio clutched his forearms and pushed back.

But he didn't loosen them.

"Stay still, Clio," he said in a harsh whisper that had goose bumps rolling over the exposed skin at her neck.

Furious and confused and so many things that she didn't have a name for, Clio pushed again. Her legs tangled with his and she fell back against him.

A shudder racked through her.

He was a cocoon of heat and hard muscle behind her. His fingers, splayed on her hips, burned through the flimsy silk of her dress.

Molten heat drenched her inside out, turning her blood into drugged honey.

He engulfed her every sense and she had never felt more like sinking.

"Do not tease a fire in me that you're in no way equipped to handle, *bella*," he whispered, before he licked the rim of her ear. "I'm not particularly fond of celibacy, especially now that I have every right in front of God and law over the one woman I've wanted so desperately for so long."

Shock waves jolted through her, spreading heat and need to the tip of every finger and toe.

His thighs were concrete columns behind hers, his midriff a steel wall. And his erection grazed her left buttock.

It was enough to jerk Clio out of the buzz.

Mouth dry, Clio jerked to the front. Or at least tried to. With one arm locking her snug against him, the other climbed up her belly, up her breasts and clasped her jaw.

Long fingers traced her lips, and she forgot how to breathe.

Stop it, please, she wanted to say but the words were consumed by the raw need coursing through her.

The blunt tip of his finger traced the cushion of her mouth. "Open that luscious mouth, Clio." She did and he pushed his finger inside.

Closing her mouth around it, Clio sucked it while her tongue laved it. Wet heat rushed between her thighs.

He cursed again, louder, harsher, and his arousal grew against the valley between her buttocks. Left her too tight inside her own skin.

She gasped as his teeth dug into the flesh at her shoulder. Pain and pleasure fused together as he licked the tender spot, his breaths coming on top of each other in a harsh rhythm.

And still, he didn't let her move. Didn't give her anything more than he decided.

He cupped her breast, and heated wetness drenched her sex. Throwing her head back, Clio pushed into his touch.

Just once, she wanted to feel his touch all over. Just once, she wanted to let it be about pleasure and only pleasure. The hardened nipple rasped hungrily against his palm, an answering pull between her thighs.

Mouth buried in her neck, he licked her skin, and Clio moved restlessly. The slide of her garter against her thighs, the rub of her own skin was torturous, her sex aching and throbbing.

With his fingers under her chin, he tipped her face up. Caught by the reflection in the oval, floor-length mirror, Clio flushed. Her eyes were droopy, her mouth trembling.

And he…he could have been cast from marble for all the expression in his eyes.

"Have you had enough, *bella*?"

Something in that mocking tone of his lit a fire in Clio. It was a fantasy to believe that he could feel anything for her—hurt or pain or desire—without allowing himself to do so, a fantasy to think she could affect him in a way he couldn't control.

A fantasy she was becoming more and more invested in, a fantasy that would break her if she didn't kill it now.

That fear sliced through the haze of desire and alcohol. "Have *you* had enough, Stefan?" she said, meeting his gaze in the mirror. She had no idea how she strung the words together, no idea how her brain even cooperated when she was aching everywhere. "Have you proved to yourself that you can have me panting in heat within a few seconds, that I'm the same as every other woman on the planet in this, too? Isn't that the game we are playing, dear husband?"

He turned her around, and still there was not a glimmer of emotion in his face.

Clio would have taken anything, even fury at this point. She wanted to crack that hardened shell he wore like armor; she wanted to shatter it and wound him. And it was the most dangerous thought she had had in her life.

"Why did you drink tonight when you never do, *bella*?"

"Because you're a mistrusting, cynical asshole who hates the very sight of me and who thinks I'm a manipulative bitch out for your millions."

"I never said that."

Clio didn't know why she was so angry, only that it was unbearable that he wasn't even moved. "Your look all evening did it for you. After that first drink, I found it was easy to not give a damn about you and your glaring and your low opinion."

"Or it could be because you know what's been building between us this past week and you're terrified to face it and you wanted an easy out.

"Whatever happened tonight, come morning, you could say, *I was out of it*."

He dissected her emotions, her decisions so easily that she felt raw, out of control, bereft of words.

He undid the golden cuff links and pushed his sleeves

back, arrogant confidence dripping from every pore. "Is the buzz evaporating yet, *cara*?"

Clio pushed him, something hot and achy clamping her throat. "I've had enough of you and your—"

"No, you haven't," he said grabbing her again. This time, she was facing him and there was nowhere to hide. "Stop hiding, Clio. Unless you stop and face it, there'll always be another situation to run from."

"I'm not—"

"You left England when you found out that your father had arranged every day of the rest of your life from what you'll study to who you'll marry. It was an incredibly brave thing to do but it was still running away.

"For all these years, you hid even when you knew Jackson was cheating you—you let him do it. Tonight, you drank because you don't know what to do with me."

He placed his hand over one breast and a gasp fell from her mouth. He covered her mouth with his and sparks cindered at her mouth spreading far and wide, making her hungry and desperate for more. "What you're doing to me, standing here like this, with desire lacing your gaze… Do you have any idea how torturous this is for me?"

And he gave her what she wanted.

He stroked and bit, nipped and laved at her mouth while she clung to him, her body, her will, her mind, all his.

"You drank because you didn't want to be responsible for this, Clio," he whispered against her swollen mouth.

Slowly, he pushed her back, creating distance between their bodies.

"For all the names the media calls me, I will not seduce you tonight and shoulder responsibility for it tomorrow while you call it a drunken mistake."

Disappointment cooled her body as neatly as if he had dumped the champagne bucket full of ice over her head. "No?"

"No. When I take a woman to bed, it's not out of pity or shame or joy or anger. It's pure lust, *bella*."

"So you won't finish what you've started, then?"

"Not unless you speak the words." In an intimate gesture that set fire to her skin, he tugged the delicate neckline with rough fingers. It gave in with a tear and a rasp—thousands of dollars and ripped now. The upper swell of her breast bared to his slumberous gaze. He bent his arrogant head and pressed a hot kiss to the flesh. Nipped it with his teeth.

Need knotted at her nipples, making them achy and tight. Her sex pulsed, wet and aching.

Clio had never known such liquid desire, as if her skin and sinew was all filled with want. Want for him. Want for the one man she shouldn't want.

Want for the man who had given her everything, but really nothing.

"Tell me that you want me to tear that dress off of you completely, *bella*." Anger colored his words. "Tell me to run my hands and mouth over every inch of your skin, tell me to sink into your heat until it is all either of us can feel." Contempt punctured the heat in his words. "Tell me to give us both the relief that we're both so desperately craving.

"Tell me and your every wish will be my command, *bella*."

Utter resignation reverberated in the way he held her loosely against him, in the way he sighed against her willing flesh. And it was that resignation, that shuddering exhale as if he was giving in to the inevitable even as he hated it, that cleared the haze from Clio's head.

Had she known that this moment was coming? Was this the only way she could think of having him, when she could absolve herself of all responsibility? Was this how she had let Jackson walk all over her?

Would she always let life happen to her, rather than take charge of it?

Shame cooled her skin, leaving her shaking. Tugging

the torn lace of her dress upward, she stumbled back. Her breathing out of sync, she tried to collect her aroused senses together.

She wanted to be held and kissed and touched by him so much that it was a cavernous chasm inside her.

But not like this.

No. This was not fair to either of them.

She looked up and met his glittering gaze, every inch of her vibrating with need. "When I look back at this night a decade later, I want to remember something else other than your self-disgust that you want me and my desperate attempt to escape it, as you put it so well."

"Clio—"

"Yes you do, Stefan. You hate that you want me when it isn't your will, don't you?" She blinked, striving for strength. "I want to have one thing that will make me proud about today. I want you to leave. Thank you for saving me from myself once again."

The flesh over the angular bones of his face, already so lean and spare, tightened even further, until he was all jutting angles and brooding arrogance. He went still, inch by inch, ridding himself of that glittering want and desire, ridding himself of any emotion.

That growing stillness in him, that willpower in action— it was the most disconcerting thing she had ever seen.

"As you wish," he said with one lingering look before he turned and left.

She could almost believe that her words had pierced him. Almost.

Roughly tugging at the bodice of a dress that could have probably fed a starving family for a few months, Clio sank to the bed and covered her face.

As caustic as his analysis of her life had been, Stefan had stopped them from making an irrevocable mistake.

She should be glad for it. All she needed was to convince herself of it.

* * *

Standing under the ice-cold shower spray, Stefan shivered. His teeth chattered in his mouth, his skin grew goose bumps. If he looked down, he would probably see that his balls had forever turned blue.

But even the possibility of permanent damage to his manhood couldn't erase the picture of his wife from his mind.

He had never seen a more beautiful woman. Her vulnerability shone in her eyes, her desire too pure and real to be anything but temptation, her struggle to be better than herself a wonder for him to watch.

Neither could he curb the small flicker of warmth in his chest.

Was this what Clio would do for him?

Punish him, torture him and yet push him toward being a better man than he had been this past decade?

That he had resisted her, that he hadn't given in to his need and taken what she had so freely offered, that he had protected her, even from himself, he would count as a win; he would count it as a little bit of honor still left in him.

CHAPTER NINE

WHEN CLIO OPENED her eyes the next morning, there was a hammer and a pointy needle inside her skull, *and* someone had pulled the silky curtains aside to let in reams of sunlight to punish her with.

Or at least, that's how it felt.

Clutching her head, she turned to her side and groaned. Tears prickled behind her eyes at the dull, pounding ache through the top of her head.

Her mouth was dry, and her throat parched. She tried opening her eyes again and was about to sit up when a strong arm pulled her up with infinite gentleness.

A whimper erupted from her throat as a blend of lime and aftershave and masculine musk teased her nostrils. It was like a slap to her senses, at once decadent and eviscerating…

Just like the man was.

She stiffened in his hold but he didn't relent.

Of all the unholy, damnedest things in the world, why did Stefan have to be up before her on the first morning of their ill-conceived marriage? Why couldn't she have started it by setting an unaffected tone, one that she wanted?

"Buon giorno, cara."

The honeyed words boomeranged against her skull as if he had shouted them.

Another moan escaped her and a smile curved that sinful mouth.

Thick wet hair fell onto his forehead. His freshly shaved

jaw glinted, and he smelled clean and nice and as sinful as the red-velvet cake she had devoured last night.

Bastardo, she mouthed the word that she had heard Alessandra use.

His gorgeous green eyes glittered with humor, his smile so beautiful that her chest hurt.

"Go away," she said, hiding her face in the pillow, super-aware of her messy hair, parched mouth and her old Columbia T-shirt that constituted her nightwear.

"Take this," he said, opening his palm to a white pill—her migraine medication—and a glass of water in the other hand.

Too far gone with the ache in her head to even offer a token protest, Clio grabbed the glass and ingested the pill. She lay back down gingerly, any sudden movement piercing her head.

His handsome face filling her vision, Stefan straightened the cotton duvet around her and tucked it to her chin. Tapped her nose with his finger, and pushed her hair back from her temples. "Sleep, *cara*," he whispered.

Sleep and exhaustion hit her in waves and Clio decided the concern she had heard in his voice had to be a side effect of her medication.

The next morning, Stefan awoke in his bed with the smell of coffee teasing him awake. It took him a few seconds to figure out why he had a feeling that he had missed something. He looked at the alarm clock on the nightstand, which said eight in the morning. The red digits burned his brain.

He hadn't checked on Clio in a few hours.

Pushing back the covers, he leaped from the bed and walked through the corridor to her bedroom.

He came to a halt as he found it empty with the bed neatly made up.

The scent of gardenias clung to the air and before he knew it, his lungs were filled with it. Running a hand

through his hair, he leaned against the entrance, a wisp of
something keeping him in the room.

A hairbrush lay on the dresser opposite the bed, and a
pair of jeans and a silk top neatly folded on the bed.

A strange quiver gripped his abdomen to see the bed
empty of her tall, athletic form after seeing her there all
day yesterday. She had refused to even eat anything, only
asking for water again and again. Silently bearing it as if it
were her punishment. Looking at him with eyes wide with
shock as he checked on her every couple of hours.

Why are you checking on me? she had asked once, her
eyes drugged with sleep.

Did she think him so heartless that she was shocked at
such a small act of concern? Had he given her a reason to
think differently? Why did he care?

Irritated at how scattered his thoughts were, he walked
back to the kitchen, following the smell of coffee.

He came to an abrupt halt at the unusual scene in front
of him.

Clio stood at the counter, her back to him, unpacking
breakfast, he assumed, from the mouthwatering smell.

She was dressed in dark blue jeans that hugged her long
legs from ankles to her trim waist and a sleeveless white
silk shirt that showed off her tanned arms.

Her hair fell straight to her waist, a river of ambers and
reds, glinting where sunlight struck it.

He watched in rising fascination as she slid the lid off
one plastic box, grabbed a fork and popped a piece into
her mouth.

Pancakes and maple syrup, mouthwatering bacon and
coffee—his favorite meal from back when they had been
at university. They had all teased him because he would eat
it for breakfast, lunch and dinner.

Her face turned toward the French doors, she closed her
eyes and let out a long moan as she chewed. A drop of syrup
stuck to the side of her mouth and she licked it off with an-

other satisfied little groan. Color suffused her cheeks as she repeated the ritual.

Bemused and turned on, Stefan watched as the pleasure she wrought from the little ritual rendered him stupefied.

The next time she picked up another piece with her fork, it took everything he possessed to not join her and direct her fork to his mouth. Or not to taste the syrup on her lips.

"The suite comes with a butler on call twenty-four hours, Clio," he said, pushing off the wall and walking into the kitchen. "You don't have to arrange our meals, *bella*."

Her fork clanged on the counter, the tinkering sound of it filling the silence.

She turned and watched him with those big eyes, color climbing up her neck.

The silk blouse was so sheer that he could see the outline of her bra, and the dip of her waist. It was so strange how so many small things about her he observed, his fascination arising from the most mundane of moments.

Like the delicate turn of her wrist and the blue veins there, like the crooked slant of her nose, the way she grabbed her hair away from her face with both hands and roughly pulled it back thrusting her breasts up…

Dannazione, the woman was lethal in how quickly she made him think of sex and skin.

Shrugging, she stepped back as he advanced. "I actually wanted to cook breakfast as a thank-you," she muttered. "But this state-of-the-art kitchen doesn't even have sugar and milk. So I walked a bit and grabbed breakfast."

"A thank-you? Why?"

Her expression was straightforward, her shrug a bit too casual. "For looking after me yesterday."

"Do they always last that long?" he said, thinking of how she had held her head. For a couple of hours, he hadn't left her side, a tenderness he had forgotten he had possessed keeping him there instead of ordering the staff to help.

It had been a long time since he had done something so

simple and satisfying as looking after someone. He used to do it all the time.

Another of his innate traits that he had buried deep.

"Kind of, yeah." Another shrug. "This whole week has been very stressful and then I didn't eat anything the whole day of the wedding and then guzzled down that champagne, so it was kind of like inviting the demons to play inside my skull."

"Why was it stressful? Didn't the wedding planner take care of everything?" he said, covering the distance between them.

The closer he moved to her, the heavier his blood flew in his veins. Just the scent of her soap and skin...it set up an instant reaction in him.

Blinking rapidly, she clutched the counter behind her. Which stiffened her posture and thrust her small breasts up.

"You're joking, right?"

"Why were you stressed, *bella*?"

"Because I was getting married under the strangest conditions that I ever dreamed of and the beast I was marrying thought I had trapped him into it," she said, thunder filling her voice.

He grinned. "The beast?"

"Yes. Anyway, I know that our contract doesn't stipulate looking after each other in case of migraines brought on by stupid decisions and showing concern toward each other, so I'm really grateful to you for—"

"Shut up, Clio," he said, staggered at how easily she had him swinging from mood to mood, like a damn monkey being operated by a switch.

Just fifteen minutes into the day, he had felt a strange warmth in his gut at the way she occupied every inch of the suite that had always been free of feminine intrusion, had given him unrivaled morning wood just by standing in his kitchen and now he was annoyed as hell.

At her and at himself.

All he wanted to do right now was tear up the bloody contract, pick her up, carry her to his bedroom, and peel that denim off of her slowly, inch by inch until he could touch her all over.

"Is the migraine gone now?"

"Yes, thank you," she said primly.

Was it his arrogance that rankled at being dismissed so well? Or was it the allure of a woman who didn't immediately fall for him?

Chewing on that errant thought, he picked up one of the coffee cups and took a sip.

The bitter brew on his tongue instantly reminded him of his home, a home he hadn't visited in so long. "You found a Sicilian blend in Manhattan?" he said, surprised.

A flush claimed her cheeks at his pointed question. "I know a Sicilian coffee stand. I go there every once in a while."

"My favorite breakfast *and* coffee. *Grazie*, Clio." Leaning next to her, he tried to corral the various emotions exploding inside. Clearing his throat, he offered her an awkward smile. "Take the day easy. Go to the spa or if you want, I can have the pilot take you to…"

Her face fell. "I have no other machinations behind bringing breakfast for you except to say thank-you, Stefan."

Beneath the caustic tone there was a thread of hurt that struck a chord in him.

Should he be so satisfied that she cared what he thought?

Even as he had stood under the icy jet of his shower on his wedding night, his shredded control an astounding concept in itself, there had been a strange exultation in knowing that he had been the reason she had drunk.

A sadistic streak that he now possessed apparently, in addition to being a mistrusting asshole.

Dio, the woman was turning him inside out.

"I was just surprised, Clio."

"Because I brought you breakfast? Is that really such a

hard thing to grasp that I would want to do something so mundane for you? Are you going to weigh and give a price to every little exchange between us as long as we are stuck with each other?"

Stuck with each other?

That very phrase riled him up to no end.

He had moved so close to her that he could see the green of her eyes darken, could see the pulse in her neck flutter unevenly, could hear the way her breath fell short. "*Dio, bella.* Shut up or I swear—"

"Or what? Will you add another clause to the contract that I can't speak unless you give me permission—"

Grabbing her slender shoulders, Stefan slammed her to him and kissed her. It was the best thing to start the morning with.

With a gasp, she fell against him, anchoring her hands on his chest.

Shaping her head with his fingers, Stefan slanted her mouth and nibbled at it, his desire slowly spiraling out of control.

She tasted of syrup and coffee, sweet and bitter, like fresh desire and old memories all blended together to drive him to distraction. The scent of gardenias entered his bloodstream and teased his senses.

He groaned as she sank her fingers into his hair. Turned into stone as she sank those teeth into his lower lip.

If only he could finish what they started in the kitchen…

He couldn't think of one reason why he couldn't take his wife to bed. Or why kissing her first thing in the morning, in a domestic setting that should have given him hives, felt so natural.

If they continued this way—kissing and nibbling and pressed flush against each other—it wouldn't be long before he had her trapped beneath him and thrusting into her wet heat on that huge bed in his room.

The thought, instead of scaring her to her senses, painted such a vivid, erotic picture that Clio whimpered against Stefan's mouth.

The hands shaping her hips and her bottom with a possessive grip instantly relented, a breath of air blowing over her tingling lips. "*Merda*, Clio. What am I going to do with you?" his ragged whisper snagged onto her senses. "We should have included a clause for this, *bella*."

Somehow, Clio found the sheerest thread of self-preservation and hid her face in his shoulder. His skin was like heated velvet—the muscles beneath tensing.

It had been a flippant thing for her to think the thought about including sex in their contract. But to hear him actually say it, to see that he couldn't think of anything between them as anything but a transaction, it punched her in the gut like a blow she hadn't seen coming.

Did he really think no more of her than any other woman? And if he did, why did she care?

Before he could enslave her with his mouth again, she moved away around the breakfast bar and leaned against the wall.

Her legs trembled, her breath felt as if it would never be normal again, but she had finally put distance between them. And judging by how his eyes glittered, it was no small feat.

"Clio—"

She pushed away the need in her to one corner, the cascading hurt to another.

"I know that the media focus is going to be on us for a little longer, but I still would like to be more than your arm candy and apparently, 'the recipient of scorn and envy of a number of your ex-girlfriends'," she said quoting from one article she had read today.

All she had done was scan the internet for world news as was her habit with coffee. Instead, she had opened the

Pandora's box of Stefan Bianco's exes and their reaction about his wedding.

It was a long list comprising models, actresses and singers that even a pretend wife could get insecure about.

He frowned, looking at her as though she had sprouted another head. *"Mi scusi?"*

It seemed walking away from his embrace cost her every brain cell she possessed. The man kissed like he did everything—with absolute dedication. Her lips still tingled, her breasts felt heavy and her entire body was one pealing mass of sensation.

Marshaling her thoughts, she began again. "I'm beginning Phase One of my reincarnation, beginning a life that's not defined by whose wife or fiancée I am. I have received a couple of callbacks on some jobs I applied to. Hopefully…"

He started shaking his head and her words trailed off. "Not necessary, I—"

"If you make one comment about me *mooching* off of you—"

Thunder danced in his eyes. "Keep that delectable mouth closed, *cara*, or I know of a very enjoyable way now to do it for you. Christian told me just last week that the charity the four of us runs needs a manager. I think you'd be a good fit for it."

Clio blinked and stared. "Are you serious?"

"Dio, bella! Why are you so doubtful about your own abilities? Where is the woman who thought everything in life was a challenge she had to rise to?"

Clio flinched. More at the fact that she had no answer rather than from his tone.

He clasped her cheeks and lifted her chin. His gaze was awash in tenderness. The unexpected gentling of his mouth mocked her doubts. "Yes, I'm serious. I would never tease you about this, Clio.

"Instead of turning your back on all those connections your name brings, instead of turning away from the powerful friends you have, instead of stubbornly refusing your new status as my wife, use them, *bella*.

"Use them to further your career, use them to help someone who's never had the advantages we had, use them to make whatever you want of yourself, Clio.

"You've already conquered the hardest obstacle by staying the course on what we started, by showing Jackson what you're made of."

"But I swore to make something of myself, Stefan. If I—"

"Nothing will come of all the resources and connections of your family and background if you aren't smart enough to channel them properly, Clio."

A lightness filling her, Clio wrapped her arms around her waist. She wanted to hug him so bad. But he wouldn't like it.

"That is, after and *if* you ever find something on Jackson."

"I will," Clio said with utter confidence. "It's just a matter of time."

"Then make that time now, Clio. As long as we carry on this pretense, you already have a full-time job of being my adoring wife."

"*Believe me*, it's not easy to remember the adoring part," she quipped.

With a deft aim, he threw a plastic spoon at her.

The way his eyes lit up, he reminded her of when he had been so carefree and affectionate and open. The memory that smile brought was so strong that she stared at him greedily.

"My board members and their wives are dying to meet you. And my assistant tells me we've been invited to several dinners and charity galas, in and out of New York."

"I should probably charge you for making me into a glorified escort."

"I think escorts provide other services, *bella*." He sent her such a scorching look that Clio should have combusted on the spot. "Are you offering?"

"Do you want to start our fairy-tale marriage with domestic assault, Bianco?"

He grinned and it was like her own personal sun had dawned in the living room, filling her with his warmth inside out. "No, Mrs. Bianco," he countered smoothly. "I'd like to start it with a kiss from my wife."

Robbed of speech, Clio stared back. It shouldn't bother her. It was just a technicality. He was teasing her.

Still, the words clung to her like a physical brand on her skin.

Apparently satisfied that he had shocked her, he forked a piece of pancake into his mouth. The usually scornful curve of his mouth relaxed with a sigh.

"It's not my fault that they all want to meet you. Apparently, you're an asset any sensible man would be lucky to have."

"Of course. Let's not forget how valuable my blue blood and where I come from are. Because there couldn't be any other reason in the world that a man would want me, right?"

"Do not put words in my mouth, *bella*. But I will tell you this because you seem to be forgetting it. It took guts to tie yourself to me, Clio. If you didn't know it before, you know it now, *sì*? I will give you nothing but what you have rightfully earned from me.

"Yet you didn't back off. It took guts to start on the path to reclaim yourself. It took guts to take a stand on what matters to you when Jackson used those filthy words for you.

"You're far stronger than you give yourself credit for. Now find something on Jackson during the day while you dazzle the world as my wife at night."

Clio stared at his back, his words ringing in her ears.

He was right. That decision had entirely been hers. But only two days in, she wondered if it was more dangerous than courageous.

Dazzle the world was what they did and they did it so well that even Clio couldn't tell where the pretense ended and where reality began.

Charity galas and dinners with influential, powerful men from all over the world, sometimes in New York, once in Hong Kong and once in London—from visiting art galleries to the charity-sponsored schools and shelters all over the world.

And everywhere they went—big or small—the media followed them.

In just a couple of weeks, Clio and Stefan had been almost around the world aboard his private jet and had become the media's favorite couple to talk about.

Frustrated more than once about hitting a wall with Jackson's financials, Clio had taken to alternately learning as much as she could about the charity that Rocco, Christian, Stefan and Zayed had set up to help underprivileged kids in so many cities complete degrees through scholarships and find jobs.

The range and scope of the charity stole her breath. It made her immensely proud to learn of the continuing resources and time all four of them poured into it and excited her beyond limit that she could be a part of something so fulfilling.

And wherever Stefan and she landed after their marriage, she wanted to be a part of it for the rest of her life, could see herself carve a path through it.

In a weird twist of fate, she was enjoying the pretend life with Stefan more than she had enjoyed her real one with Jackson for three years, even though it was essentially the same kind of life—jet-setting, networking, showing off, making and breaking deals over dinner and drinks.

The man at the center of it, however, made all the difference.

Being around Stefan was like being caught in the orbit of a star—invigorating and exciting. And it made her never want to leave. Everywhere she went, she saw acquaintances—some she had known through Jackson—but it seemed like a foregone conclusion that, of course,

Stefan was the victor in some fight against Jackson, and she the spoils.

She knew she shouldn't feel pleasure at that so much, but as Stefan had said, Clio was going to take every small victory. Because the one time they had run into Jackson, he hadn't dared meet her eyes, much less utter a word.

Only the price she paid for that felt increasingly high.

The most luxurious and spacious suite in one of the finest hotels in New York wasn't big enough for the both of them.

She felt Stefan's restlessness at being caged in the suite like a physical force, sensed a loneliness that had hardened into a shell around his emotions.

The only time there were flashes of the old Stefan was when one of his three friends was present. It was the only time she saw genuine laughter in his face.

And the more she saw of this new Stefan, the more she wanted to shatter that shell.

Despite knowing that it was the last thing she should be doing, she couldn't stop from trying. She had already contacted his parents, was counting the minutes to when they would arrive in New York.

Was desperately praying that he wouldn't throw her out of that suite the moment he saw them.

"Your wife is the most beautiful creature I have ever seen," his fifty-seven-year-old accounts manager gushed and Stefan barely stifled the urge to punch the man's ruddy face. The old lech had already pawed at Clio when Stefan had introduced her.

Smiling at him, which took quite a considerable effect, he turned away from the man, leaving him midsentence.

"Ready to go home?" he whispered, reaching Clio.

Flinching at the palm resting against her lower back, Clio covered up the wariness in her eyes.

Before she could reply, Stefan's cell buzzed and he checked the identity of the caller.

It was the hospital where his assistant, Marco, was still struggling for his life. His gaze fell on Jackson in the crowd just as he switched his phone on.

Two minutes into the conversation, grief knocked the breath out of his throat. Turned his gut into an aching chasm.

Not trusting his temper, he marched into the balcony and pushed his fist into the wall. Even the pain that radiated from his knuckles and up his arm was not enough to blunt the pain of losing Marco.

"Stefan?"

He heard more than saw Clio's hurried steps in the darkness, felt her search for his hand. Distress filled her gaze as she pulled his arm to better see his knuckles.

Her gasp resonated in the lush night. "I have a first-aid kit in the car. Let's go." He had a feeling she was barely keeping the tears away.

"No," Stefan roared, pulling his hand away from her. He had no idea what he would say or do to her. "Leave, Clio. Instruct the chauffeur to drive you home."

The stubborn woman stayed right where she was, a resolute tint to her chin. "I'm not going anywhere. Not until you tell me why you rammed your fist into the wall like a—" a catch in her throat "—Stefan, please. Tell me what's going on."

"My executive assistant, a man who's been there with me for ten years, through every up and down, he was swindled by Jackson."

He saw her disbelief in her stunned look. "This man… he was not just an employee?"

Somehow, she had reached the crux of the matter. "No. Marco…he started out with me when I began investing in real estate. He was so loyal and caring that he became important to me, despite the bastard I became. Strange, huh?"

A small smile curved her mouth. "Not really. How much can you deny your own nature, Stefan?" She looked away for a second. "What happened to Marco?"

"He tried to kill himself and was hospitalized. Today, he died, leaving his little girl without a father. A little girl, *bella*…and that scum is still free to enjoy his caviar out there."

Instantly, she threw her arms around him. But Stefan saw how pale she had turned. Saw the flash of guilt in her eyes as if she was responsible for Jackson's actions. Which was why he hadn't told her so far.

She had enough burden of her own to carry.

"I'm so sorry, Stefan. I…don't know what to say."

Untangling himself from her, Stefan looked away. "He did the same to me years ago, Clio.

"It was a year after Serena left. I had struck gold with a few investment ventures and I realized the luxury real estate market was huge and I wanted a big chunk of it.

"I did extensive research and acquired stock in a small trading company. For months, I slogged round the clock, put everything I had into this one venture.

"In just a matter of minutes, the stock I purchased crashed, all the money I invested in it went down the drain. And I was back at square one.

"It was the lowest point of my life. I had lost everything after Serena left, and to be knocked back like that…it made me question everything.

"If it wasn't for Rocco and Christian and Zayed anchoring me, if it wasn't for the fact that my father had always taught me to stand up after one of life's knocks, that would have been me."

"I'm so sorry for your friend, Stefan. But that would never be you. God, I can't even bear the thought."

"I have to stop him, Clio."

Nodding, she wiped her cheeks roughly. "We will, Stefan. I promise."

Just as his arms relaxed around her, just as he found the knot in his gut loosening, she stepped away from him. "I'll…I will leave you alone. See you later."

"Running away again, *bella*?" he asked with a mocking smile. "For days now, you have avoided meeting my gaze. You touch me, you smile at me, you kiss me when we are in public and the moment it's just us, you...can't wait to run away. How long are we going to continue like this, Clio?"

Her steps faltered and she looked around.

"I won't let you turn sex into a transaction, Stefan. I won't join the leagues of women who have slid into this slot you have for them. And you and me..."

"What about you and me, *cara*?"

"I let one man lock me in a relationship for everything but the right reason. Wanting you, being near you, not touching you, it's a lesson in itself," she said, shocking him with her honesty.

Her gaze glittered with a power he hadn't seen. The way she looked at him—all consuming and without hiding anything—knocked his breath again and in a completely different way. A wave of desire, laced with something else, buckled him.

"But I can't give in, Stefan. I can't just have sex with you and pretend like nothing has changed between us."

Stefan watched in rising fascination and frustration as she walked away without looking back.

Something had changed in her, and something had changed between them.

He didn't know what. Only that he couldn't hide from the truth she had so neatly pointed out.

Turning away, he stared into the dark night. He would never be able to reduce Clio into another nameless woman that satisfied his body.

He hadn't even told the other three how defeated he had felt when he had lost what he had made because of Jackson. How close he had come to giving up and going home in shame to his parents.

Clio made it so easy to depend on her, to confide in her. Even her censure somehow changed him.

He was so desperate to touch her, to brand her, to claim her as his in the most intimate way possible. He couldn't breathe in that cage without seeing her stamp everywhere.

To tangle with his wife would mean relearning himself because Clio wouldn't leave him untouched. And that was a risk he couldn't take.

CHAPTER TEN

THREE WEEKS AFTER their wedding, Stefan had the usual early-morning online meeting with most of his executives around the world. The scent of freshly brewed coffee, which Clio religiously picked up, dragged him into the kitchen as it did every day.

He poured himself a cup, took a sip and watched Clio at the dining table, poring over a bunch of documents and making notes.

A frown tied her brow, her face was rapt, reminding him of the time they had crammed for an exam together years ago.

Suddenly, he felt a burst of warmth in his chest at the sight of her, an almost forgotten sensation.

It had become a ritual—one among numerous others that they had fallen into when they returned to New York between trips around the world.

Sharing a cup of coffee, looking through Jackson's financials, discussing new initiatives for the charity, and the best of them all for him personally—rediscovering all the little offbeat eateries in different corners of New York they had all used to favor back when they had been at university.

He frowned, suddenly seeing the pattern, the determination with which Clio had dragged him against his will the first couple of times. As if she wanted to erase all the bitterness of his love affair with Serena, the bitterness he had let corrupt his memories of New York and the happy years he had spent here, the aversion he had developed to settling down in one place or making meaningful connections with anyone.

As if she wanted to remind him of his true nature, of the parts of himself he had destroyed to move on in life.

That he hadn't recognized her intentions until now showed how deep he was into their farce of a relationship.

He was about to interrupt her when he heard the elevator doors open with a swish at the entrance to the suite, followed by familiar voices. Clio instantly went still, the knuckles of the fingers clutching the pink ballpoint pen becoming white.

Feeling an uncomfortable knot in his gut, Stefan made his way through the corridor into the lounge and stared wordlessly.

Wearing a beaming smile, his mother practically ran toward him. Threw her petite form into his arms, uncaring whether he caught her or not.

As it had been for a decade, shame sideswiped Stefan, robbing his ability to speak.

His father, tall and broad like Stefan, was more remote, watching him silently.

He hadn't seen his father in almost a decade and his mother only a couple of years ago when she had traveled to Villa Mondelli, his friend Rocco's house in Milan, to see Stefan.

Tears flowing over her cheeks, his mother launched into a rapid dialogue just as Clio arrived from the lounge.

His father, a traditional and usually reticent man, moved toward Clio and grasped her hand in his. Studied her with a mixture of curiosity and warmth. "You're as beautiful as you are generous, *bella*."

The familiarity his father showed Clio stunned Stefan, rendering him mute.

Her face suffused with warmth, Clio was shaking her

head. Her hands trembled, her gaze resolutely turned away from Stefan. "It's nothing, Mr. Bianco. I was just doing my duty."

Duty?

"Thank you for inviting us to your home, Clio," his mother said in heavily accented English from the circle of his arms.

"You have to excuse us, it's not a proper home," replied Clio, looking anywhere but at him.

"But home is where your heart is, *si*?" his mother said, fresh tears filling her eyes again.

His head swapped between Clio and his parents as if he was at a tennis match, shock literally robbing him of coherent speech.

A decade ago, he had tried to convince his parents of the same thing—that he had fallen in love with Serena and that he wanted to stay back in New York.

They had been so against it that they had threatened to cut him off and he, so naive, so desperate to be in love, had told them he was fine with that.

But Serena had wanted nothing to do with him without his parents' fortune.

"We would have loved to come for the wedding but it was not to be," his mother piped up again, glossing over the fact that he had not invited them.

Except for phone calls, he hadn't been able to even meet his father in the eye.

"He's fortunate, to have such a loving wife." This was said to his father.

"Please, come in," Clio finally said, her voice hoarse. "Did you have a safe flight?"

"Yes," his mother replied. "Aboard Stefano's luxury jet means we don't need anything."

Shock shuddering through him, he grasped Clio's wrist and tugged her toward him.

"I have to call the butler and have some food arranged for them," she said, tugging her hand back.

"How long will you run, *bella*?" he whispered before his mother commanded his attention again.

He felt the shiver that racked through her slender frame. The little minx had arranged everything, even commanded his pilot without his knowledge.

All Stefan wanted to do right then was to excuse himself from his parents, drag his wife inside and demand an explanation. Or maybe ravish her first and demand explanations later.

Because his desire for his alluring wife seemed to be the only constant thing in his life these days.

After a dinner of expertly prepared *pasta con le sarde* and *impanata di pesce spada*, swordfish pie, his favorite, which Clio had requested the butler learn and cook for dinner, and lots of colorful conversation—which had been mainly his mother's curious questions about how they had fallen in love, the wedding and when they were planning *bambini*, and Clio's deftly spun tales for answers—the silence in the cavernous lounge jarred on Stefan's nerves.

Every time he had visited New York over the past decade, he had stayed in the same suite at the Chatsfield. Now it was as if a volcano had erupted all over his life and there was no way he could contain the damage being done, couldn't turn it back into the safe, sterile place it had been just a month ago.

His father's hand on his shoulder prodded him out of his thoughts. "You're angry with your wife for inviting us."

Stefan shook his head in automatic denial before he caught a flicker of understanding in his father's eyes. His father had never lied to him, had never done anything but love Stefan.

"You know we would have welcomed you back all these years." Not even a hint of hesitation could be heard in his father's voice. "Why have you not returned to Palermo even once? Why have you stayed at a distance, Stefano?"

The unhidden ache in the question came at Stefan like a sharp punch, ripping through the shell he had built around himself.

Had he known, somewhere, that his father, of all the people in the world, could sense how changed he was from the inside? Had he been afraid that his father could see that there was nothing good left in his son after what Serena had done?

"Was it to punish us for threatening to cut you off all those years ago? Have you become such a cruel man, then?"

"No," the denial waved out of him. His father would accept nothing but truth. For the first time in years, Stefan looked inward.

"What kind of a man keeps away from a mother who dreams of holding her son in her arms again?"

To hear that painful resignation in his father's voice was Stefan's undoing. Words rushed out of him on a wave of guilt and shame and so much more that he had locked up for so many years. "Serena…she took my very belief in myself when she left me. In just one day, I became a stranger to myself. I didn't know myself and I could not face you as a failure. I…was not worthy of you and Mamma after choosing such a woman over you. How could I face you after I had so selfishly shattered all your dreams?"

Understanding dawned in his father's gaze. "And all these years? After you built your empire, after you proved to yourself that you could succeed?"

Stefan shook his head, a lump in his throat. He had no answer for his father.

"Has she taken everything that was good and kind about you, too?"

She hadn't. He'd given it all up willingly. He hadn't wanted anything that could have made him vulnerable like that again. Along with his naïveté, he had also given up his heart.

After everything he had done to wipe her from his life, he had still let her win.

The realization clawed in his gut. He had held on to her rejection, had held on to the poison she had spewed into his life for so long.

Had let her corrupt everything that had been good and pure in his life even though he had been determined to prove her wrong.

He had denied himself and his parents the joy of seeing each other.

Clutching his father's hands, Stefan spoke. "I have let my shame and guilt stop me from visiting you these years…I wanted to prove myself worthy of you again and in the process, I forgot what you taught me…I forgot everything that is important in life."

Nodding, his father patted his back. "Your mother, she does not see things. But I would have been immensely sad to see my son become like this…if it were not for your Clio, Stefano. To see you with a woman like that, it makes my heart easy."

What would his father say if he knew it was nothing but a farce? What was stopping him from making the woman he wanted with an insane hunger his own? The thought erupted on the heels of the first one.

The elevator swished open and his parents left, beaming smiles on their faces.

Instantly, Clio excused herself and Stefan let her run away for now.

The way he felt right now, it was better she stayed away until he was more in control of himself and his emotions.

All day, his parents had commented on how well Clio and he suited each other, had been ecstatic at every small exchange between them.

Hadn't been able to keep their eyes off Clio as they went sightseeing into the city. Had demanded Clio and Stefan show them the Columbia University campus, all the spots that the media had dug up and built their love story around.

His mother had pronounced proudly that Stefan and Clio's marriage would last longer than her own marriage of forty years, that they would continue the tradition of a long, happily married life as the Biancos always did.

His mother's comment opened up a wound he had resolutely patched up long ago, an ache that could consume him if he let it.

Because he could never trust another woman, never reach for that happiness ever again.

And try as he did to ruthlessly remove that small part of him that wanted a fantasy to come true, Clio kept igniting it, kept pushing him toward the path where nothing but pain awaited him.

Even the happiness he had spied in his parents' eyes demanded a high price of him.

Clio had unnecessarily brought his parents into their pretense, cruelly shown him glimpses of a future that could never be his.

And that she made him want it again was unbearable.

Closing the door behind her, Clio entered her bedroom.

Anticipated fear churned through her gut. Her fingers slipping on the keys of her laptop, she typed in her password and looked up her bank account.

Sweat running down her back, she pulled a sheaf of papers she had left on her nightstand.

Jackson's financials…

Her gut folded in on itself as she finally pinpointed the discrepancy she had been trying to find, and the tremendous truth of her financial affairs rammed home.

Jackson had robbed her of every last penny, literally…

This was proof enough for the Securities and Exchange Commission to investigate Jackson. Proof enough to pull everything on him…

Her legs gave out under her and she sagged to the cushioned chair in front of the vanity, her breaths rushing on top of each other. Why it had finally come to her today, at this moment after weeks of trying, she had no idea.

Today when she had seen a real smile curve Stefan's mouth, today when she had seen the flash of pure joy in his eyes...

Today when it seemed like she had made a difference in his life.

This was all Stefan needed from her, why he had agreed to her deal, why he had married her... And once he had it...

Clutching the chocolate-and-gold veneer of the table, she leaned her forehead to it, trying to lock the tears in her throat.

The whole day had been the upward ride of a roller coaster—going higher and higher on the tale she had spun about Stefan and her, the pressure building. Until this moment when she was crashing down.

Rosa Bianco looking fondly at Stefan and her, and weaving dreams for their future life, had been the same as looking at a reality that was even better than the one she had wanted for so long, one that she was living every day, but was still out of her grasp.

Pretending to be the woman Stefan adored was like a drug she never wanted to quit, that could distort her reality and delude her. Still, she didn't want to give him the proof yet.

"You shouldn't have interfered, Clio."

Stefan's voice behind her simmered with anger and emotion.

But she had done what she had intended. She had finally gotten past that shell of his.

She had to face the music now, but for his sake, she would do the same again.

"Turn around and face me. There's nowhere to run tonight."

Warning vibrated in his tone, along with arrogance. And instead of scaring her, it goaded Clio. Someone had to show Stefan what he had become, had to remind him what he used to be.

Still seated, she turned around to face him.

"I didn't interfere, Stefan. Nor do I have any intention of running away."

"No? Because I have a feeling you're taking our vows literally, *bella*. Everything that you have been doing these past two weeks, everything you think I need, you can stop it. You have no *duty* toward me, Clio."

He spat the word as if it was a curse, as if he couldn't stand the idea of her doing anything in the name of it. Her muscles quivering, Clio frowned.

It was as if there were two parts of her within—one wanted to back down, apologize before the tension in the room exploded, one wanted to challenge him about her place in his life, wanted to hurt him as he did her.

For what else was the tightness in her chest?

Uncoiling from the chair, she straightened her spine. "Maybe I have no duty toward you as a wife, Stefan. God knows nothing but that bloody contract defines that between us. But what about as a friend who wants to do something for you, who wants to see you smile again?"

He prowled into the room and into her space. Long fingers wrapped around her nape possessively. "I have three friends—ones who don't interfere in my personal life. I don't need another friend."

"So everything you have done for me then, what—?"

"That's a different matter."

Clio half snorted, half laughed, her temper getting the better of her again. "Can you hear yourself? You gave me the right to interfere in your life when you interfered in mine. Goose and gander, Stefan."

"You've lost me again. But do not repeat this, Clio. Or I

have to forget my own rules, too, and they are already very muddy right now."

"They were over the moon to see you, Stefan. And I know that it meant something to you, too."

Scorn filled his gaze. "Then why didn't you invite yours, *bella*?"

Burying the hurt that instantly swarmed to the surface, Clio shrugged. "I did invite them. I thought a farce it might be, but this is the only wedding I'll have. My mother said, *I hope you fare better with him than you did with the American.* They have no interest in my life, Stefan. Not after I walked away from the one they decided on for me.

"But having seen your parents today, I don't regret what I did. They adore you, Stefan. To not invite them to the wedding…"

His mouth tightened.

"To reject something so good and pure, this is not you."

"I doubted your reasons for wanting to marry me. I made you sign a filthy contract. Have you still not learnt who I am now, Clio?

"The naive, romantic Stefan you remember is long dead. In its place, there's only poison, Clio, poison that will destroy you. I'm warning you, *bella*…leave me alone."

His jaw concrete, he growled a sound of such utter pain that her gut twisted.

"Do you realize what you've done by involving my parents in this? They think the sun rises with you now. What happens when this is all over? How will I face them with another failure in hand? How will I explain your absence in my life, *bella*?"

That he still thought in such rigid terms should have brought Clio down with a thud. That he didn't even indulge the thought of some kind of future together, when it was a path she kept getting pulled into, should have stopped her.

"I don't know how you will. We came together to ruin Jackson. Can your parents' happiness not be the one good thing that comes out of this, Stefan? Does our marriage have to leave only destruction in its wake?"

Because that's how it felt right now.

Stefan had already helped her gain her self-respect, her strength, back but he was also going to steal a part of her. The damage, it seemed, was already done.

How could she stay away from him when he was so gorgeous and kind and honorable? When her heart gave a little leap when she saw him every morning? When her throat ached at the way he shut his emotions off as if he couldn't bear them?

She walked over to him and wrapped her arms around his unforgiving form, hid her face in his shoulder. She felt as if she was standing on the precipice of a cliff, wanted to give in and jump so much that she was feverish from it.

He tensed instantly, his grip on her arms bruising, poised to push her away.

Slowly, Clio settled into his embrace, the hard contours and sharp angles of his body pressing and pushing her own soft curves, until they fit perfectly. Heat and hardness—his maleness made her feel so secure, and wanted.

His arms came around her finally, and her breath left her in a long whoosh. His hands moved and roamed over her back, as though he was testing their fit, too, and then came to rest around her waist. Left scorching heat on her bare flesh between her top and jeans.

Warm air from his exhale coated her skin. "Thank you for bringing them here. For bringing such wonderful smiles to their faces."

Warmth exploded in her chest and she struggled to contain it. Nodding, Clio wrapped herself even tighter around him. "You have to let me in, Stefan. Just a tiny little bit."

"Tiny little bit, *bella*? You're like a stubborn virus." His smile against her temple took the bite out of his words.

She had no name for what was happening. Only that,

after years of unhappiness and misery, she had smiled so much these past few weeks, she was happy with herself.

She felt a sense of power over her own life, over her emotions she hadn't felt in so long. She would tell him about the proof, but for these few minutes, she wanted it to be only about them.

"We have no expectations of each other, which means we won't hurt each other either." His heart thudded under her hands. Out of the mess she had made of her life, it seemed there was still one good thing. "We are safe from each other."

He smiled, baring his teeth like a predator. "Are we, *bella*? Because every minute of every day, I feel like I'm on the edge. You smile at me, you tease me, you rile me, you challenge everything I think of you, of myself, of the world. And now, my dear wife, you're meddling in my life. Safe is the last thing I am with you around."

Bending that arrogant head, he breathed the words into her temple, her scalp prickling at the way his finger tugged her hair.

"And what I do want, *so desperately crave from you*," his free hand moved up her midriff and rested in the valley between her breasts with his hot mouth buried in her neck, "you won't grant me, *bella*." Speech slurring, he licked the fluttering pulse. "It feels like I've waited my entire life to make love to you, Clio."

Her spine melted, liquid fire licking along her nerves. She was sinking in desire and she clutched him with her arms, his body a welcoming cocoon.

"You're seducing me with words, Bianco," she managed huskily with the few brain cells that were still functioning.

"Me seduce you, *bella*?" His solid frame shook with laughter, sending ripples through her. He dug his teeth into the skin at her shoulder and bit.

Wetness drenching her sex, Clio shuddered as pain gave way to pleasure so intense.

With his arm around her, he absorbed the quivers in her body, locking her against him.

"For someone who scowls and argues that I have defined everything between us by that contract, you have me in your thrall, Clio. Quite the power trip for you, no?"

A smile tugged at her mouth and Clio gave in. Desire and joy flooded her, a honeyed combination.

That he didn't resent the desire between them—it was a step forward.

She knew how he wanted to define and restrict their relationship. He was allowed to do anything for her, but she…her every action concerning him, every word to him, he would scrutinize it. Either attach a price tag to it or reject it as unwanted.

But she couldn't not do it, she couldn't stop trying.

Whatever they presented to the world, Clio wanted, *needed* something real between them. And it seemed it could be nothing but this desire, this fire that consumed them.

She reached up within the circle of his arms and vined her arms around his nape. Pressed her mouth to the corner of his and breathed deeply. His skin, rough and stubbly, scratched her soft mouth, heavenly in its contrast. The taste and scent of him exploded on her lips, urging her to press closer and tighter. "I want it clear that this is not a power trip or a transaction or a bloody clause in your contract, Bianco."

His hands kneaded her hips, pulled her closer until his erection, a hard length, pressed boldly against just above her sex. Her mouth dried, her breath lodged in her throat.

"*Sì.*"

"I want it clear that I'm doing this because it's you."

"No gratitude, *bella*. I don't want to be your thank-you f—"

"No," she said, covering his mouth with hers. "It's because you're the most gorgeous man I've ever seen and because…I can't breathe if you stop kissing me."

His eyes glittered. "*Dio, bella.* You'll be the death of me."

Rough fingers kneaded her butt while his tongue licked the pulse at her throat. Sinking her fingers into his hair, Clio tugged hard until he lifted his head and met her gaze, until the vein in his temple throbbed, until the sculpted planes of his face stood out in stark contrast.

"Kiss me, please."

Make me feel like I can do this right. Make me whole again in this, too, she wanted to say, but held back the words, shame and fear locking them deep down.

She kissed his jaw this time. With an urgency and courage she had never known before, she pulled the lapels of his shirt until the buttons popped and flew.

Sank her hands under his shirt. Felt his heated skin and the tensile muscles. Heard the rough exhale fall from his lips. Bent and finally tasted his skin, licked his flat nipple, dragged her teeth over his skin, marking him, tasting him, until his fingers were this short of hurting in her hair, until his hard body was shuddering around her. Until his control was in tatters just as hers was.

Salt and tang and desire, he tasted so good on her lips, and he was all hers.

At least, for tonight.

CHAPTER ELEVEN

SHE LOOKED LIKE a queen, imperial, so poised, and yet she was trembling in his arms. Her pink mouth was already swollen with his kisses, her eyes drugged and hazy.

It was his wildest fantasies come true and it was much better than he had imagined.

Picking her up, Stefan carried her through the lounge.

Her hair flowing behind her, she laughed. "The bed in my room works fine, Stefan."

"*Sì*, it does. But it's not mine, *bella*. I have spent, it seems like countless nights, tossing and turning, and thinking of you on my sheets. Once we're through in my bedroom," he said, "we can go back to your room, Clio. Or that beckoning vanity in the bathroom. Or the chaise longue on the balcony overlooking the glittering skyline of Manhattan. Or the terrace where you can see the sky while I lick my way down your body."

A flush overtaking her, her eyelashes flickering down, she clung to him, trembling.

That she blushed only made his blood heavier in his veins. "*Dio*, Clio. How can you be this sensuality-personified and still blush, *bella*?"

As they stepped over the threshold into his bedroom, he slid her to her feet, her eyes rounded in her oval face.

Her gaze traveled around the room—took in the views of Central Park on one side, over to the king bed on the other side.

Grabbing the remote, Stefan turned on the lights to full. She turned toward him, her neck and cheeks still pink, a sudden shyness in her gaze.

Reaching her, he pulled her to him softly. That Jackson put those shadows in her eyes, his blood boiled just thinking about it.

"Clio, *bella*?"

She swallowed and raised her gaze to him. "Can we turn off the lights, Stefan?"

His first instinct was to refuse, to tell her that he demanded all of her, that she couldn't hide herself from him, that she was his, scars or flaws and all.

He noted the vulnerability in her stance. Suppressed all his macho claims and nodded. Stared at her hungrily until every inch of her was burned in his brain. And turned off the lights.

Cupped her cheeks and brought her mouth to his.

With her expression hidden from him, with her face only visible in strips and flashes of the moonlight, with her curves accessible to him only through touch, every other sense became intense.

The scent of her, the rasp of her breath, the tremble of her chin…he was engulfed by her, ensnared.

He kissed and stroked her lips, tangled with her tongue until the roar of his own blood was the only thing he could hear.

The hot drag of her lips over his, the hesitant slide of her tongue against his, the honeyed taste of hers, it was a feast he couldn't get enough of.

Kissing a woman until now had never been more than a forerunner to release, never more than foreplay. And yet, he could kiss Clio for hours, hear the soft mews and moans that fell from her mouth for days. Could lose himself in her soft mouth for aeons.

He would never have enough of this fantasy-turned-reality that shredded his control. He would never have enough of *her*, something warned him. He would never be satisfied with possessing her, yelled the cavernous chasm inside him.

He could never keep her from pervading his life, his days, his every moment, his every breath.

She was already everywhere, making him ache, making him want, pushing him toward the man he vowed he'd never be again. Shattering through the shell he had grown and reaching the most vulnerable part of him.

Soon, she would know all of him, she would know his darkest fear.

She would know how he had turned against his own nature and buried his heart and his deepest desires so that he could move on in life. She would know how much he envied Rocco for finding the woman who adored him for who he was in Olivia, and Christian for the family he would have with the lovely Alessandra...

How in the process of putting himself together after Serena's betrayal, he'd lost something fundamentally good in himself, how he didn't even know how undeserving and out of control he felt as he had watched Clio struggle with her fears and insecurities and emerge victorious.

How she made him wish he could be that old Stefan again.

But even through the aching vulnerability that he despised so much, he couldn't walk away.

Instead, it fused with desire, pumping powerlessness through him.

Her soft gasp when he dug his teeth into her lip sharply dragged him from the edge of his own desire, remonstrated his lack of control.

He had bedded numerous women over the decade, and yet nothing like this need today had even touched him. He craved so much more with Clio.

Of her scent, of her skin, of her aroused gasps. She was

vined around him, her slender body arching and pressing, as he devoured her mouth again.

One hand sank into her hair to hold her immobile for him, while the other snaked around her hip, pressing her into his erection.

Whatever he did to arouse her, to drive her out of her mind, he was the one who felt owned by her, consumed by his need for her. And it was a feeling he couldn't shrug off.

All he seemed capable of was drowning and that's what he did. But if he was going to sink, she would, too.

His mouth was so hard and perfect over hers. And so desperate and urgent. Her lower lip still stung, radiating waves of pain and pleasure all over, awakening a million nerve cells that had been dormant in her until now.

At least, that's how it felt.

He was hers. Clio couldn't stop the thought from resonating like a drum inside her head.

He was hers like he had never been anyone's, she knew it from the increasingly erotic strokes of his tongue.

His mouth was an erotic lesson, a blast of heat to every inch of her, a fire that spread to every tip.

"*Dio, bella.* I knew not being able to see you would be a punishment. But not in this way," he said angrily.

But Clio didn't care why or how. All she cared was that he sounded on edge. Winding her arms tighter around his nape, she pressed herself closer, tighter, relishing the hard give of his muscles. Rubbed herself against him until her breasts were crushed and her breath a chore.

He growled in response, dug his fingers into her hips in a bruising grip and swept her up into his arms.

Settling her on the high bed, he moved between her legs. Grabbed the edges of her silk blouse and pulled.

The pearl buttons flew in all directions.

The urgency in him, instead of scaring her, filled her with power. That she could send his muscled body to shudder, that she could send him to desperate need, it was a balm over wounds Jackson had inflicted so cruelly.

She looked down the same time as he did.

Her flesh was milky white in the moonlight, her nipples tight points of need against her silky bra.

His pithy curse as he traced a long finger against the seam of her bra was a song to her ears.

But instead of touching her as she ached to be, he pulled her to her knees and unzipped her jeans. Tugged them down past her thighs, and feet. Threw them across the room and settled her on the bed again.

Until she sat in front of him in a thong and bra, her bare legs stretched indecently to make space for his broad frame, exposing the heart of her.

But she sat still, the dark of the night giving her a courage she wouldn't have had if his hungry gaze settled on her. She hated that Jackson was still there in her fears when he shouldn't be, she hated that she had let him break her confidence.

"Stefan?" she called out to him, only now sensing his stillness.

Grasping her ankles, he pushed her onto the bed. And she slid soundlessly on the luxurious goose down sheets.

In the next blink, the lights came on and he leaned over her lower body in a movement of such sheer perfection that Clio forgot the glare of lights.

His gaze swept over her like a white-hot flame, inciting little sparks wherever it touched. With a gasp, she moved to cover her sex but he grabbed her hands, held them over her head, liquid lust and resolve dancing in his green gaze.

"I won't let him take away even a single part of you that should be mine today, *bella*." He sounded ravaged and angry and determined, all at the same time. "I won't let that bastard be a silent specter in this room between us."

Her heart slammed so violently against her rib cage that Clio shivered. That he could read her fears so well made her feel more exposed than her most intimate parts on display for him.

He ran a reverent finger over her rib cage to the hairline over her sex. And Clio caught the moan that wanted to hurtle out. "I can't bear it if you—"

"You're so breathtakingly beautiful, Clio, more so than my imagination could do justice. *Dio*, why would you hide yourself from me? Why would you deny me the pleasure of seeing you when you know how much I want you?"

Clio tucked her face away from his, shameful tears filling hers.

He trailed hot kisses along the seam of her bra, kissed the curve of one breast, and she shifted restlessly. She needed his hands on her breasts, needed to feel his mouth over the tight, aching points.

But, of course, he wouldn't give her what she wanted unless she stripped herself bare of that last layer. Until she was completely exposed to him.

Until she was all his.

His hand caressed the flesh of her hips, tugging her close, until he was leaning over her and she was looking up at him. "Tell me."

"I was not hiding myself. I was hoping to not see your reaction, Stefan."

With a hard grip, he turned her to face him. "Explain."

"No."

"Yes."

Being naked in front of him should have made her awkward. But the maddening circles he drew over her hips, the protective circle of his arms, freed Clio from that last fear. "He...I have been unhappy for a while. With myself, my career and, of course, my relationship with Jackson. I...somehow found myself without friends even. And it affected everything I did. How I dressed, how I ate, how I interacted with others. Even..."

"Sex?" He gritted out the word as though the very thought of Jackson and her set his teeth on edge.

"Yes. It became such a chore that one night he said the Hudson River in winter would be more warm and receptive. After that, I kept finding excuses to not do it. That he cheated on me so blatantly and for so long is unforgivable but I can't help thinking I pushed him to it. That it was something in me.

"I don't want to see the same disappointment in your face, Stefan. If the lights were off, I could still lie to myself about…"

To bare this last fear of hers felt so excruciating that her words died on her lips. Clutching her eyes closed, she waited with her breath hinging unevenly in her throat.

Seconds piled on top of each other but he said nothing.

Until Clio felt his fingers crawl up her thighs, and part the folds of her sex.

Invasive, arousing and utterly addictive, he pressed the bundle of nerves that had been aching for his attention with his thumb. Drew on it in mind-numbing strokes.

Her spine arched, her breath flew out of her in a wave. A lick of heat swept through her as he kissed the sensitive skin of her thigh, as she felt the warmth of his breath.

"You smell so divine, *bella*." In one smooth move, he pushed two fingers inside and Clio gasped at the avalanche of sensation. "And, *dannazione*, you're so wet for me."

Turning toward him, Clio met his gaze, heat pooling under her skin in a rush, blasting through every tip.

Bending over, he tasted her mouth. Palmed the engorged and needy tip of one breast.

Clio moaned into his mouth.

"I was not joking, Clio. I have always wanted you, even back then."

Surprise glinted in her face. "Hitting on every woman you met was your knee-jerk response."

"I have always wanted you. And now, the reality of having you in my bed…you have no idea how crazy you drive me, Clio."

While Clio grappled with that information, he bent his dark head and sucked her nipple.

Raw sensation zigzagging over her, Clio sank her hands into his hair and arched into him, needing more.

With a smile, he continued the rhythmic pull of his mouth, driving her out of her skin, while his other hand delved between her curls down below and started a fire again.

He stroked and palmed her heat while suckling at her nipple. The relentless caresses even as he whispered the wickedest words in her ear started Clio on a chase that knocked the breath out of her lungs.

There was nothing but sensation and pleasure, beating at her from every side. There was nothing but Stefan—his kisses, his touches, his body's warmth and the best of all, his words.

And Clio forgot all her fears, all her doubts as her climax hit her in wave after wave, throwing her out of her body. She felt like she had been shattered and then remade.

Tears seeped out of her eyes.

Feeling his gaze on her, she opened them and saw his raptured look. Gasped when he pulled her onto his lap and took her mouth in a bruising kiss.

But she wanted more, she wanted to be utterly possessed by him.

She ran her hands over his chest, traced the ridges of his ribs, learned his skin to her heart's content. Reveled in his short breaths, the flexing of his muscles to the slightest of her touches.

Reaching down, she unbuckled his belt and pulled it out. Unfastened his trousers and sneaked her hand in.

Felt the already engorged length of him grow harder and longer in her palm.

Rubbed her thighs together as the heat that rushed through her at the rigid weight in her hand.

Coming to a kneeling position, she vined her arms around him, and licked the rim of his ear. "What else did I do in this fantasy?"

His muscled frame racked in her arms, and she felt like the most powerful woman on earth.

"Some other time, *bella*," he whispered back, his abrasive palms roaming restlessly over her back.

"Now, Bianco," she commanded, and bent down to lick his flat nipple.

His hands tightened in her hair, whether to hold her there or push her, she had no idea. Kissing the ropes of muscle that had fascinated her for so many weeks, she looked up and caught the flush in his cheeks.

Saw the truth shining in his hungry gaze.

Grinning, she trailed wet kisses down his rock-hard frame. The muscles tensed harder and harder as she moved downward.

The tip of his erection lay against his taut belly.

Clamping her thighs together at the thrill in her own blood, Clio licked the soft head.

His harsh groan fell on her ears, a thunderous roar that goaded her on.

On the next breath, Clio fisted her hand at the base and took him in her mouth.

Tasted the hard length of him in a long suck that sent little tremors to her own sex. She continued as he shuddered beneath her caresses, as he cursed and groaned.

"Now this feels like quite the power trip, Bianco," she whispered, and before she could breathe again, she was on her stomach on the bed.

"We will see who has the power, *bella*," he threw at her, before he pulled her onto all fours.

On the next breath, he held her hips still, and thrust into her wet heat.

Closing her eyes, she made a ragged sound that ripped from her. His hand snaked out under her, and kneaded a heavy breast as he set a rhythm that left her with no thoughts of power.

Only sensation remained. Only he and she remained, joined together in the most intimate of bonds.

And as he pushed her onto her release and found his own, only pleasure remained.

Not contracts, not shadows of old fears, nothing but the man who was a perfect fit for her. Nothing but the man who had awakened every part of her.

"I found the proof today, Stefan," Clio whispered, as she lay supine in Stefan's arms. Maybe it was the fact that after a long time, she felt completely at peace. That she felt secure about herself, about the direction her life was heading in.

Even if the future was still an enigma.

Maybe it was just the fact that the man who held her to him so tightly with his arms around her, as if he couldn't let go, had made love to her so well that the postcoital haze had lent her false courage.

The thing she knew for sure was that she wanted to tell him. She couldn't remove his pain about losing a friend of so many years, but she could at least give him the satisfaction of bringing Jackson to justice at last.

Stefan stilled behind her. It was so complete that she wondered if he breathed anymore. Suddenly, his arm around her felt like a lead weight.

"I have lost every penny I had." The words rushed out of her haphazardly, the weight of saying them out loud stunning her anew.

"What, *bella*?"

The sheets rustling around her, Clio lifted his arm and turned around. Caught the resigned look in his eyes just as he blinked and chased it away.

With the gears in her head running finally, understanding dawned in her.

She swallowed the knot of hurt in her throat that felt like glass. He had thought she was commenting on the state of her funds, asking for a handout in a roundabout way.

Kicking into a sitting position, he pulled her up, until she was sitting by his side on the enormous bed. When he looked at her again, there was nothing but curiosity. "What are you talking about, Clio? If you need money, all you have to—"

Clio stopped his words with her palm over his mouth, before he could deal her more than a surface scratch. It was his automatic reaction to any question, from any woman regarding money, she pacified herself.

He had made a conscious decision to ask her politely about it instead of seething with distrust and contempt.

It was a step forward in their fragile relationship.

That was the best she was going to get from him.

Pulling her hand into his, he laced their fingers together and kissed the back of her palm. "Clio?"

Shaking her head to chase away her stupid misgivings, Clio offered him a small smile.

"I'm sorry. It hadn't quite sunk in and saying it out loud finally did."

With his finger under her chin, he tilted her face up. "Clio, I want honesty between us, *bella*. Above everything else. That's how this began," his knuckles tapped her chin, "and that's how I would like us to continue."

Her stupid, grasping, desperately greedy mind latched onto the fact that he wanted this, *whatever this was*, to continue.

She was on a slippery slope in this relationship they had now, and yet, she wasn't scared or afraid.

All she cared about right now was that he wanted her, in his life, in whatever capacity it was. Her heart thudded so loud it was a wonder he didn't hear it. "Of course. Do you remember I told all you guys about my aunt Grace once?"

"The one who hated your parents and vice versa?"

Smiling, Clio nodded. "She had always been sweet to me when I was growing up. She died a couple of years after I came to Columbia. I went to her funeral and found out that she had bequeathed me a bit of money. I think it was her way of high-fiving me for walking away from everything that my parents had wanted for me."

Stefan grinned. "Sounds like a sweet lady."

"She was. You should have heard her swearing. She did it like a sailor. Anyway, it took a few years for the legalities to go through and I received the money a year after we graduated. About twenty-five thousand pounds."

Pushing back from her, Stefan stared at her. "But if you had that much cash in hand, why did you have to borrow from Christian? Why not use it to secure your rent or to pay off your school debts?"

"Because my parents knew that Aunt Grace had bequeathed me that money. My mother even commented that for all the claims I had made, I was happily taking handouts. So I locked it up in a secured bond, determined to make it in New York through my way.

"And when I was broke, it was better being obligated to Christian than letting them learn that I needed help."

"You are a stubborn woman, *bella*. Isn't it enough you turned your back on such a prestigious family and started a new life halfway across the world?"

"Why didn't you go back to your parents after Serena left? Why start from scratch, Stefan?"

Thunder dawned in his gaze. "I don't want to talk about her."

"We're talking about what made us who we are today." Kneeling in front of him, she clasped his cheeks when he would have moved away. "We're talking about you and me, no one else."

Tension seethed in his shoulders but Clio held on to him. "Serena walked away from me because I was nothing without my parents' fortune. She made me question my very belief in myself. I was determined to prove her wrong, determined to make the fortune she wanted all on my own. Pride and shame, *bella*, I was drowning in them so much that I hurt my parents for so many years."

The flash of pain that wreathed his features pierced through her. That it could still affect him so much…

"After all these years, do you not still realize it is her loss, Stefan? To walk away from you because your parents disowned you, to leave a man like you behind…"

God, he had loved that undeserving woman so much, with all of his heart. To have a man like Stefan love her unconditionally like that… Clio couldn't imagine what it could even be like. The very thought had such a mesmeric, compelling quality to it that her entire being resonated with it.

She kissed his mouth, heat and tenderness and affection and a hundred other things rushing out of her on a wave she couldn't curtail. "That woman was a first-class moron, if I may say so."

A smile curved his mouth. "Wow… Are you sure you don't need to wash out your mouth?"

"Oh, don't encourage me, Bianco. It could get a lot dirtier, believe me. The reason I liked Aunt Grace so much was because she had no problem cursing in front of kids either."

"I can't wait, *bella*."

Clio laughed against his mouth, a river of joy flooding her.

As if it was as natural as drawing breath, he captured her mouth with his. Molten heat uncoiled in every nerve, every muscle. It was as if her body knew what he could give, and craved it.

Tongues dueling, lips scraping against teeth, in a matter of seconds, they were both breathing hard.

Somehow, Clio had climbed into his lap and was straddling his erection. With a moan, she moved, the crease of her sex rubbing against his, sending erotic tingles through her lower belly.

Cursing, Stefan locked her hips before she could do it again. Color bled into his cheekbones, his nostrils flaring. "As much as I would love nothing but to be inside your wet heat, *bella*, I want to hear your story more."

Sighing dramatically, Clio smiled. "Oh, to be denied sex for a story... Your libido and prowess has been overestimated by the media, Bianco."

He bit her lower lip as punishment and a hundred nerves jangled within Clio. "The sooner you tell me, the sooner you can have me, Mrs. Bianco." His grin was so natural, so filled with that openness he had possessed so long ago that her breath caught in her throat. "Any way you want."

"Fine. But don't forget your promise."

It was the first time he had actually smiled after a conversation about Serena and the poison she had spewed in his life. For that smile, she could give up all the money in the world.

Clio hugged the fact to herself like a proud accomplishment.

"What about the money your aunt Grace bequeathed you, *bella*?"

Knowing that his mood was going to worsen, Clio slipped off him and got to her feet. "I met Jackson a few years later. Until then I put Aunt Grace's money in a CD that I couldn't break for five years. It had matured a year after I met him. And he talked me into investing it in his hedge fund company."

The room went from warm to ice-cold in a matter of seconds.

Uncoiling his huge frame from the bed, Stefan reached her. "And?"

"I have known it for a while at the back of my mind from the bits and pieces I have heard him mutter about over the last year. And I have seen proof of it now. He lost most of the investors' money."

"That's a risk you take with hedge funds, *bella*." Pulling her to him, he wrapped his arms around her. "I'm so sorry you lost the money she gave you, Clio. I'm sorry he deceived you in so many ways."

Clio went into his embrace as if it was the most natural thing in the world to do. And the fact that he had done something nonsexual and intimate without reservation, it blunted the shock of realizing another level to Jackson's deception.

That something her aunt had given her out of love was now lost to her hurt more than the fact that she was basically penniless. Again.

"That's not it. From all the claims he made, and the returns he's been showing in his statements, my investment should have grown by leaps and bounds."

She went back to her bedroom and grabbed the files. He was heading into the kitchen, so she laid them on the table. After a few seconds of rifling through it, he stared at her with icy fury in his eyes.

"These records show your investment had nearly fifty percent returns. But the actuality is that he's lost it all? He's fronting the funds from somewhere else?"

"Looks like it," Clio whispered.

Instantly, she was lifted off the ground in a bear hug. "You did it, *bella*. You found it." Putting her down, he cradled her face in his palms. "That's all we need to expose him, *bella*. Jackson won't recover from this."

"It doesn't feel like an achievement, Stefan. I have a sick feeling in my gut. Everything he did, everything he ever said to me, it was all such a big lie. How can I ever—"

She was more than surprised when he pulled out a dining chair and pulled her onto his lap. His long fingers tracing the angles of her face, he pressed a kiss to her temple. Held her within the cocoon of his embrace. "Shh… It's all his shame, Clio. Not yours."

It was a place Clio never wanted to leave, and the want was so visceral that she shivered.

* * *

Holding Clio in his arms as she trembled, seeing the pain in her beautiful gaze abate as he kissed the lush curve of her mouth, Stefan finally felt at peace after a long time.

Strange since seeing his parents after so long, unburdening his shame and guilt with his father, and making love to Clio, the day should have been an emotional roller coaster.

Yet the facts that Clio had uncovered about Jackson, that he finally had a chance to bring him to justice for all the wrongs he had done to so many people, freed something inside him.

He couldn't find it in him to be angry with Clio anymore for interfering. Instead, he felt grateful.

With her actions, she had only shown him how much power he had given Serena's rejection over his very life. And yet here she was, struggling to find herself again after Jackson had stolen so much from her.

In the face of her strength, Stefan felt some of his own bitterness melt. He lifted her and carried her back to her bedroom, drenched in the realization that a small part of him could trust a woman again.

However their marriage had started, it seemed he had a wife who bore his name with care and honor and duty.

CHAPTER TWELVE

Two WEEKS LATER, Stefan and Clio arrived in Gazbiyaa, Zayed's desert kingdom, the evening before Zayed's wedding was to take place. The desert palace glittered in the setting sun, breathtakingly beautiful, a haven of luxury amidst the stark landscape of the desert.

Stefan and she had been shown to a suite in the wing of the palace that was away from the festivities of the wedding and provided privacy, just as Rocco and Olivia, and Christian and Alessandra had been.

With Stefan catching up with Rocco and Christian, and feeling a bit fragile to face the other women yet, Clio toured the Gazbiyan palace with a bevy of maids—at least the portions that she was allowed to without infringing on the customs of a kingdom that clung to its traditional roots. A kingdom that Zayed was determined to pull away from the brink of war with its neighboring nation.

Everywhere she looked, there were festivities going on with a pulse of joy beneath them.

The next evening, reunited with Rocco's wife, Olivia—they had bonded over her and Stefan's kissing scandal at Christian's wedding—and Alessandra, who was beginning to show a growing baby bump, she visited Nadia, Zayed's intended.

Even as Stefan and she were taking part in Zayed's extravagant wedding, back home in New York, Jackson was under investigation by the SEC. The guilt she had initially felt had eased as more and more of Jackson's illegal business practices began to come into light.

Driven by greed, he had fleeced so many people.

Under Stefan's expert guidance on all things related to the charity and its finances, she had hit the ground running in terms of her work. When he looked at her now, there was nothing but admiration and respect in his gaze.

She had achieved everything she had set out to do when she had stumbled into his suite at the Chatsfield with her life in tatters.

As much as she had feared ruining their fragile relationship, making love with Stefan was the most natural path they could have taken.

More than a week went by where they lost themselves in learning, exploring each other, where Stefan, as if determined to be the only man in her thoughts, seduced her so thoroughly that Clio felt like a new woman in her own skin, free to embrace her wants and desires.

And the more she let herself go with Stefan, the tighter he bound her to him with his own desires. Sometimes he would wake her up with kisses, make love to her so slowly, with such thorough care that she thought her heart would burst out from his tenderness.

Other times, his desire was touched by a desperate passion that shredded his control, that had once had him taking her against the wall in the lounge, seconds after he had returned from burying Marco.

I needed you so desperately, bella, *that a week has never felt more like a lifetime.*

At those times, she felt like she wouldn't be able to breathe if he stopped.

The different depths to his desire left Clio addicted and just as desperate as him. And terrified that he was slowly, but irrevocably stealing a part of her soul.

Because as demanding and giving as he was when it came to sex, he didn't say a word to her out of that context.

She had begged to go accompany him to Marco's funeral, wanted to share the ache of that moment with him. But he had stubbornly denied her.

It was as if he could communicate with her only through sex.

Now, as she dressed for Zayed's wedding, Clio trembled when the gold silk caftan slid over her skin with a whispered caress, imagining Stefan taking it off her. She remembered the heat of his erotic promises, the addictive strokes of his tongue at her core, the sinuously abrasive texture of his skin, the whipcord strength of his thighs...

It was as if he was spreading through her every cell, every thought until he was a permanent part of her.

Grabbing her hairbrush, Clio ran it through her hair and met her reflection.

He deftly alleviated her concerns and yet didn't give anything of himself that he didn't want to.

The default pattern of their relationship.

As they stood witness to Zayed's own wedding, amidst the noise, extravagant pomp and celebration, amidst the acres of garden and incredible feasts unlike anything she had ever seen, Clio finally pinpointed the root of the growing panic within her.

It was the uncertainty of what tomorrow with Stefan would bring.

And yet, she didn't dare ask him where they were headed or what he wanted. Couldn't bear to hear him say they were done with each other. Not yet.

As usual, every small thing she required, from the elaborate, long-sleeved designer dress to the jewelry that would go with it; from the gold-colored sandals to her bangles; everything had been arranged as it suited to Mrs. Bianco's status.

He would give her everything but would he give her even a little piece of his heart? How long was she willing to let this uncertainty hang over her?

And how had she, *again*, found herself in that very spot where her happiness, her entire sense of self hung precariously on the whims of a man, and one who had ruthlessly warned her that he had nothing to give her?

Stefan pocketed the sheaf of papers that he had collected from the printer in Zayed's office and stepped out into the enormous gardens in front of the majestic Gazbiyan palace.

The most extraordinary stunts were being performed in honor of Zayed's wedding and yet the flutter of excitement in his gut felt stranger than anything he had seen.

For the first time in years, he felt as if he could have a different kind of life, felt as if Clio could fill the void he had been determined to ignore.

Burying Marco who had had such a long and wonderful future ahead had made him think hard about his own life.

He could never love Clio, never be the man who believed in it. But he wanted a future with her. And just the prospect of taking his wife home and making love to her in their bed…it was the best thing he had looked forward to in a long time.

Spotting her, Stefan laced his fingers through hers.

"Boys' club dispatched for the night?" she said with a smile.

He nodded, without bothering to clarify that he hadn't been with Rocco or Christian. Or that he had been cooped up all day in the office that Zayed had lent him, on a phone call with his lawyer. Or that he hadn't slept a wink in over a week deciding what to do.

Pulling her close to his side, he let his hand wander over her hip just as the sky burst into a million colors.

A chorus of laughter and shouts erupted from the crowd.

"You were hard to find after the wedding ceremony, *bella*," he whispered at her ear. "Almost as if you were avoiding me."

Slowly, the tension in her lithe frame dissolved. Reach-

ing a hand up, she pushed a lock of hair away from his forehead. The intimate gesture pierced through Stefan, finding
a vulnerable spot.

Her mouth tightened and then relaxed. Slowly, she pulled
herself back and looked around. "I just wanted some time
to think."

Stefan hooked their arms and tugged her away from the
festivities.

When she didn't budge, he turned around.

There was a wariness in her eyes that he didn't like.
Knew it was there because of him, because he had kept her
at a distance the past couple of weeks.

"I want to stay back for a little while more."

Fighting the first urge to let her be, because there was
something in her tone, in the look in her eyes that prickled
his skin, he clasped her face. "I told a guard I was looking
for a woman with hair the color of fire, and eyes like emeralds and skin like the softest rose. Told him that she was
the most poised, the most breathtaking woman dressed in
a gold dress that floated with every step she took and that
she looked like a queen."

Shaking her head, Clio laughed. "Flattery will get you
nowhere with me, Bianco." She was laughing and yet it had
a forced quality to it. "And it's Nadia that's the Sheikha
among us. I'm the pauper, remember."

"The guard reminded me of that, the part about Nadia
at least. But said he could also understand why I would
come to that erroneous conclusion. And then pointed me
toward you."

As they reached one of the tents that were erected away
from the celebration, she dug her heels in.

"Come on, *bella*. I want to show you something." He
sounded eager, like a schoolboy, yet he couldn't control it.

It had been so long since he had looked forward to anything so much, so long since he had wanted something in
life beyond another business deal.

"I have already seen it, Bianco. And as much as I agree that it's spectacular, I don't think a tent amidst a crowd of festive and raucous Gazbiyans is the place or the time to get it on."

Laughter poured out of him, shaking his chest, loosening every muscle. When she argued further, he lifted her and brought her into the tent.

When Stefan finally put her down, Clio looked around the soaring, tented structure with her eyes wide.

The interior walls were decorated with lush Persian rugs and priceless silks. Low-slung divans with a number of pillows in vibrant colors with golden tassels sat on three sides. On the fourth was a four-poster bed with a sheer veil resting around it.

An image of Stefan and her on the bed instantly flashed in front of her eyes, an insistent pull of desire between her legs. And yet something in her also recoiled at it.

She had laughed about it outside, but inside she was trembling with anger and a powerlessness that she loathed.

Only realizing how silent he was being, she turned around and found Stefan's gaze on her. The molten desire instantly heated her skin.

When he pulled her into his arms, excitement flared, her body automatically craving more. When he buried his mouth in the crook at her neck, at the spot that drove her crazy, snuggled into her behind so tightly that his arousal pressed into her, branding her, she pushed back into his touch, needing more.

Yet, another warring emotion emerged, polluting the want. God, she had tried so hard to not ask anything of him. To hold herself aloof, to not define their relationship in any way.

Self-disgust roiled through her and she pushed away from his touch.

His head recoiled, hurt flashing in his gaze. "Clio, is something wrong?"

"No. Yes. I hate what you're doing to me. *I hate what I'm letting you do.* I hate that I can't say no when you touch me."

His mouth tight, he rolled his shoulders. "You're doing just fine now, *bella.*"

"I can't become that shadow of myself again, Stefan. You either want this thing between us, or you don't."

"That's all I have been thinking about these past weeks, Clio."

A sheaf of papers materialized in his hand, and Clio's heart sank to her gut.

It was a contract, she knew without looking at it. Another piece of paper that would define her exit from his life.

And just the thought of walking out of his life, the thought of not sharing that suite with him, the thought of not laughing with him and not loving him again sent her into a spiral of pain so acute that she shivered all over.

Oh, God, how she had fallen in love? Where was this unbearable avalanche of emotion coming from?

How was it even possible that she still possessed this much capacity to feel? What did it say about her that after everything she had been through with Jackson, she had so easily surrendered her heart to a man even more ruthless?

How was she to survive now?

She sank to one of the divans, her legs refusing to hold her up, a hollow emerging in her chest.

When Stefan joined her on the divan, she flinched. "Just spell it out for me, Stefan," she managed somehow.

"Look at me, *bella.*"

"No." She clutched her eyes closed, desperate to keep herself together. From the beginning, he had seen her at her lowest, her weakest. Now, she couldn't bear to betray herself, couldn't bear to have him look at her with pity.

Couldn't bear for him to know how irrevocably lost her heart was.

When his fingers landed on her chin, she swatted him away. "Tell me where you want me to sign, Stefan."

But he didn't let her leave. Locking her arms, he knelt on the rug before her. "Look at me, Clio. It's not what you think."

Shock pinging across every inch of her, Clio looked down at him. His face was so gorgeous that it hurt to look at him. His gaze touched her with such naked, honest desire that her heart ached.

It hurt to look at him, to touch him, to feel his heart and to know that he would never be hers.

"What do you mean?"

"I want us to start fresh, *bella*. I want to try this marriage for real."

Her heart thudded so fast that it was a wonder she didn't have a heart attack. Throat aching, she forced the words to form. "What's the catch? What are those documents?" she said, so terrified of the answer, and yet so hopeful that he would say there wasn't one.

That all he needed was her acceptance.

That all they needed was time with each other.

Her hope would cripple her if not kill her.

And Stefan crushed it under his Italian loafer when he said, "You get five hundred million dollars when you sign it."

"Five hundred million dollars? I don't understand."

"No matter what happens in the future, I want you to have security. I want you to—"

"So you don't expect us to last, then?"

"Nothing in life has guarantees, *bella*."

Nausea bubbling up her throat, Clio searched his face, wondering if he was joking. Praying that it was a nightmare she would wake up from. Hoping it was one of her migraines playing a trick on her.

Because this couldn't be happening, could it? Another

man wasn't measuring her worth, equating her love with money, was he?

"I don't get it, Stefan. You're paying me so that you can buy the trust you apparently can't show in me? Like all the celebrity couples who first draw prenups to protect their assets from each other?"

"You do not have any assets."

"Exactly. So are you protecting yourself?"

He cursed so long and loud that Clio had goose bumps on her skin. "You're completely misunderstanding this. I tore up the old contract. I hate how Jackson cheated you. I want you to never have to worry about..."

"Really? After a decade of knowing me, you think all I want is a free ride through life?"

"No. This is something I want you to have, something for my own peace of mind."

Clio shook her head, understanding dawning. She shot up from the divan, furious energy burning through her, looking for an outlet, even as a deluge of pain broke her within.

It was so easy to think it was her fault, so easy to think he was doing this because she didn't have any money, to think it was because he lacked trust in her motives, in her.

It wasn't.

It wasn't about her at all.

Stefan knew her better than any other person in the entire world. But the freeing thought only gave way to another gut-wrenching truth.

"Five hundred million dollars—is that my price tag, Bianco?" she said gasping for breath. "Because I'm sure if you have a chat with your buddy Jackson, he will tell you that I should come in a lot cheaper."

The most unholy fury dawned in his gaze. He grabbed her arms in a viselike grip, a vein throbbing in his temple. "Don't you dare talk as if Jackson and I are the same kind of man, *bella*. Don't you dare cheapen yourself."

"So the man does bleed," Clio threw at him, agonizing fury coming to her rescue.

"Stop twisting my words."

She grabbed the contract and threw it on the ground, tears falling over her cheeks. "God, you still don't get it, do you, Stefan?

"This is the price for everything we share, Stefan. This is the price for our happiness, our life together that you're talking about. You're buying me, my affection, tainting every word I would say to you, attaching a price tag to even the sex we have."

"Enough, Clio! You're reading this all wrong."

Shaking her head, she ran a hand over her cheeks. "The sad part is you don't even realize it. You're giving me money because that way anything I offer you, you already have a reason for it. Because you don't have to accept anything I give you."

"No, *bella*." His olive green gaze turned hard, untouched. "You told me you didn't want anything from me. And I told you I don't want anything from you."

"All I wanted was one sentence that you wanted this to be real between us, that you wanted to at least try. That you want to see where we could go from here."

"It is what I want, too."

"With a caveat, yes. The awful thing is I'm so anxious in here—" she rubbed her chest, as if she could relieve the tightness there "—so tempted to just sign the damn papers, to accept the little crumbs you will throw me. So in...so in love with you that I'm prepared to just take whatever little you give me. How pathetic is that?"

Stepping back from her, he looked as though she had struck him again. As though he couldn't bear to hear the weight of her confession.

As though he never wanted to set eyes on her.

As though she had stuck a knife in his back while smiling to his face.

And it was the haunted expression in his gaze, the horrified look that sealed her fate for Clio, that ripped her last thread of hope into pieces.

He would never accept her love. He would never give her his trust.

"You're not in love with me. You're deluding yourself like every other woman that has come into my bed before you. I warned you about that, *bella*."

The nasty barb landed where he intended, lacerating her, carving a nice little slice in her breastbone.

That he would throw his own past in her face, that he would dirty him and her and what they shared, only showed how much her declaration rattled him, how deeply buried his heart was.

She wished she could be furious with him, she wished she could hate him for it.

But all she felt was a keening gnawing that ate through her gut.

"I didn't think I would ever feel like this again, that I would ever want to place my happiness in another man's hands. But it's not my fault. Even with the block of ice you have for a heart, even with the poison you have held on to all these years, you're kind and funny and you're the most honorable man I've ever met."

He recoiled as though she had struck him again. "That is proof enough that you're still lost, Clio." He sounded so far away.

"No. Finally I know myself, Stefan."

"How can you forget the pain Jackson caused you? How do you even know what you...what you claim is real?"

"By putting a value on you and me, our happiness together, you have showed me how priceless I am, how all consuming and incredible my love for you is. And how little it will always mean to you, how we could do this—" she moved her hands between them "—for the next decade and you will still never give me what I want, what I deserve.

"You're my knight, Bianco, once again saving me from my own desperation. You're the best friend a girl could ask for, the best lover for a woman with tattered self-esteem. But to spend a lifetime with you…it will destroy me."

His gaze darkened, inch by inch of his face hardening as if he was willingly shutting himself down.

"Don't do this, Clio," he said, grabbing her. His mouth branded her in a fiery kiss that almost broke her resolve. Her knees melted and she clung to him as he seduced her with tenderness and passion. "We can have a good life together."

Clasping his cheeks, she pushed him back, stared at the storm gathering in his gaze. He wasn't untouched by this. But it wasn't enough. Nowhere near enough.

She was greedy, she wanted all of him.

"No."

"Stay, *bella*." Even now, he only commanded with that hard look in his eyes, even now, he held his heart locked away from her.

Even now, he scowled at her because she had dared to fall in love with him.

Smiling through the tears in her eyes, Clio shook her head. "I would have, a few hours ago. I would have danced with joy, thrown myself at you. But I can't now. I don't want your money, and I don't want the little you offer of yourself. Have a nice life, Stefan. And thank you for teaching me my own worth."

Without looking back, Clio stepped out of the tent and into the open grounds.

A thousand sounds and scents greeted her, but nothing could touch her past the audacious hope ringing through her that he would chase after her, that he would kiss her and hold her and tell her that everything would be fine. Tell her that he had made a colossal mistake and that he wanted her in his life.

That he wanted to be loved by her.

But he didn't.

And the emptiness around her only made her realize what she wanted that much harder.

She wanted the Stefan who had admitted to having a wild, reckless thing for her.

She wanted the Stefan who admired her and respected her.

She wanted the Stefan who had been one of the warmest, most openhearted men she had ever met.

She wanted to lose herself in his arms and be the woman he lost his control over.

She wanted to be the woman that made him smile, laugh and she wanted to do it for years to come.

She wanted them to be friends, lovers and so much more. She wanted the contract ripped and burned, she wanted his millions and her penury to never come into the equation between them, in any form.

She wanted it to be just her and him and their love for each other.

Clio wanted all of him, every breath and every cell, every thought and every sigh, every kiss and every touch.

And the want was so deep, so raw that it was a physical ache in her gut. That want was so desperate that she shook all over, waves of pain splintering inside her.

But this time, she would not settle. She would not let a man, even the one who she loved with every breath, define what she was worthy of.

Because she deserved all of him.

Stefan sank to the divan, reeling under Clio's angry accusations, reeling under the weight of her confession.

So in love with you...

Those words pierced him even as he recoiled at the fury that had been shining in her glittering gaze, even as he couldn't believe the truth of it.

How could she love him? How could he begin to believe

her when there was nothing to love, when he had given her nothing but pain?

How could she ruin everything by bringing that word between them?

He had no use for her love. He had nothing to give her back. And the one thing that he had wanted to give, the one gesture he had made because he cared about her, she had thrown in his face.

How could she let her claim destroy what they had?

He wanted to call it a dent to her pride, a tantrum she was throwing because he had hurt her with offering her money.

But Clio never threw tantrums and Clio didn't have any fascination with his wealth.

Clio didn't drop hints for gifts, Clio didn't ask to be introduced to his powerful friends. Clio didn't flirt with other men to make him jealous.

Clio didn't dangle sex as a bargaining chip.

In only a few weeks, Clio had made him laugh more than he had in a decade. He had lived more and for the first time in years, he had made love to a woman instead of seeking physical release.

Clio was the farthest from what Serena had been.

Clio was Clio—generous, kind and vibrant. Clio was the first woman, other than his own mother, who cared about his happiness, who cared that he smiled.

Clio had walked through the fire of his distrust and Jackson's treachery and emerged whole.

And he... *Dio*, he had treated her worse than he had treated any other woman in his life from the moment she had set foot in it. Had punished her for his own demons, put her through so much because of his own insecurities.

Because somehow, through her struggle with Jackson, through her struggles with herself, through her determination to remind him of what he had been once, Clio had become a mirror in which he saw what he had become.

The picture he saw of himself over the past few weeks, he despised it.

But it was too late.

He buried his head in hands and growled, a chasm of pain opening up in his gut. The tent reverberated with her words, her pain, with the rawness and purity of her emotions. With the darkness of his own poison, with his loneliness, with his utter desolation.

He had done just as Zayed as predicted. He had ruined the most wonderful thing that had come into his life, shattered any chance of happiness with his own hands.

All I wanted was one sentence that you wanted this to be real between us.

But he hadn't been able to ask that small thing. He hadn't been able to give her even a small part of him. He hadn't been able to take the warmth and generosity and the wonder that was Clio.

He still couldn't. He couldn't take that step and open himself to pain and agony again.

Wasn't that why he had offered her that settlement instead, even if he had realized it too late?

Even after all these years, even as he had found the perfect woman, the woman he had dreamed about his entire teenage years, the woman whom he would have loved for the rest of his life, he still couldn't take that final step, couldn't find the courage to be the man who laid out his heart.

CHAPTER THIRTEEN

ALMOST TWO MONTHS LATER, Stefan was in the midst of a meeting in his Hong Kong office when his laptop pinged. Still listening to his main accountant drone on and on about their Asian holdings, he looked at the screen and stilled.

The email was from Zayed's wife, the Sheikha of Gazbiyaa. Wondering what it was that Nadia, the deceptively strong woman his friend had married, would send him, Stefan clicked on it.

His heart pounding so hard in his chest as he viewed the thumbnail, he clicked the attachment open.

It was a shot of him and Clio the morning of Zayed's wedding that someone must have clicked unknown to them.

They were standing at one of the turreted balconies in the Gazbiyan palace, the morning sun behind them. He remembered the moment instantly.

Rocco and Olivia, Christian and Alessandra, he and Clio, and Zayed had just finished breakfast. Clio had wandered to the balcony, and as if pulled forward like a string, he had instantly joined her there.

Had covered her bare arms with his and shuddered as the scent and warmth of her had stolen into him. Had pushed the thick fall of her hair away so that he could see the delicate crook of her neck. Had loved tracing her slender hips with his hands, had loved how naturally she had fit against him.

An instant surge of yawningly desperate need claimed him and he closed his eyes.

Dio, how she would respond when he pressed his mouth at that crook…how her long fingers would rake over his skin, marking him, owning him as he pushed into her, how boldly she had looked at him that last time, binding him to her… Drenched in the memories of her, which were at the same time so vivid and yet so distant, Stefan almost reached out for her.

She hadn't flinched or pulled back that morning. Burrowing into his body, she had looked up at him and smiled.

He opened his eyes and stared greedily at the shot again.

And the shot had captured that smile.

There had been no hesitation, no artifice, no shadows in it. Everything she felt for him—it was in that smile.

It spoke of love, courage and the thing that stuck in his chest like an ice pick, open joy. It said so much about their intimacy, about how gloriously perfect that moment had been in his life.

Life with Clio would be full of such indescribable moments—of love and happiness.

In that stunning moment between powerlessness and need, it struck him how much he loved her. How he would do anything if it ensured she would always smile like that.

It was like a lightning bolt, washing away the poison that had festered in him for so long, opening the hurt inside him like an avalanche.

And that smile, that love that shone so beautifully in her eyes, that was what he had gambled away.

The voices around him sounded as if they were coming from far off. The view from the fortieth floor faded as he struggled to breathe past the tightness in his chest.

The ache in his heart, the fear in his gut, was so visceral that he rose to his feet jerkily. That moment brought all the yawning emptiness he'd felt over the past couple of months to the fore.

She had banished him from her life with such ruthless will that even he was impressed. In two months, he had

had only heard from her once—one paltry email that had stripped him of even hope.

Do not come back to New York, please. This is my home. If you ever valued me for even a minute, leave this city for me. Leave me be, Stefan.

And so he had. Against his very nature, he had left her to face the media. Left their marriage in a limbo.

Because his business empire was spread out all over the world, it had been easy to stay away.

He didn't know if she wanted a divorce. He didn't care.

He had snarled at Christian when the latter had visited him in Hong Kong, told Zayed to leave him the hell alone and had thrown himself into work. Nothing could fill the increasing chasm of his lonely days blending into endless nights, nothing could touch him past the morass of his guilt and grief and emptiness.

He had spent fifty-six days in a hell of his own making, dying to hear her voice, craving her smile, wondering if he would ever kiss her mouth again, listening to little tidbits about her from Olivia, who, he had a feeling, would love to see if he would bleed.

She was flourishing in her new position at the charity.

She had been called in connection to the SEC's case against Jackson.

She was looking good.

Every day, he broke a little more inside until there was nothing. But he couldn't be this coward anymore, he couldn't bear another day without seeing her, without holding her in his arms.

How lost had he been to slap a price on his heart?

She had been right about everything.

He had given her everything except himself.

And the woman she had grown into these past couple of months, she would settle for nothing less than all of him.

He must have said something because suddenly the conference room was empty around him.

Picking up his cell, he made a call, his heart in his throat.

His voice muddled in sleep, Rocco answered. "Stefan?"

"Where is she, Rocco?" he said without preamble

His oldest friend understood immediately. "In New York."

"I know that. But not where. I know that Olivia knows. I know that Clio went to her. I need to see her, Rocco. *Now*."

After what seemed like an eternity, Rocco sighed. "I'm sorry, Stefan. Believe it or not, my stubborn wife hasn't told even me where Clio is."

"She is your damn wife, why the hell not?"

"Because she takes standing by her friends seriously. If you want to know where Clio is, you have to ask Liv. Stefan… take care, *fratello*."

Stefan barely heard Rocco's warning. In two minutes he instructed his pilot to fuel the jet, ordered his secretary to cancel everything indefinitely.

Nothing in his life had any meaning without her.

He needed his wife, his friend, his lover back. He needed the woman who had made him live again, smile again, made him feel so much again that he couldn't breathe for the ache of it. And he would beg if that's what it took to bring her back into his life.

As Clio stared at Stefan, standing at Olivia's friend's doorstep, his face haggard and covered in stubble, his thick hair rumpled, his collar askew, her entire world tilted and shook. Her gut folded on itself, her breath balling up in her throat.

She pulled the edges of the threadbare cardigan together defensively as his perusal, hungry and invasive, continued.

Without a word, he entered the flat and closed the door

with an arrogant kick of his handmade Italian shoe. Wandered soundlessly through the small flat.

Every inch of her stilled in panic as he picked up the cardboard box she had discarded carelessly on one of the sofas.

Anger flashed in his green gaze and then cycled to fury and then to utter powerlessness. He turned the box around and around with those long fingers.

Her breath quivered in her throat noisily as she stared at the expression she thought she never would see. The box was crushed in his hand, his knuckles showing white.

"When did you take the test?" he finally said, something so desperately painful in his tone that she just stared at him.

"Clio?"

Recovering, she fought the urge to go to him. "Yesterday morning."

Another silence ensued, stretching her nerves so tight that a breath of wind could tear them apart.

"Yesterday morning…"

A quiet sound fell from his lips, shock marring his features. "And?"

The tiny room reverberated with the sound of his question, all the more unnerving for the whispered entreaty that it was.

Clio swallowed and instinctively wrapped her arms around her still-flat tummy. She had expected him to give her a display of that fierce Sicilian temper. This silently obvious conflict rattled her on so many levels. "It was positive. I made an appointment to see a doctor in two days to have it confirmed, but I…I'm pregnant."

"And you didn't think to tell me?" came the instant retort. He pushed his fingers through his hair, paced the small room. Let out a string of angry curses. Came to a standstill within touching distance, his features wreathed in torturous agony. "*Dio*, Clio… Would you have hid this from me if I hadn't come today? Would you have…"

Hands tucked in the pockets of his trousers, he turned away from her abruptly. As if he couldn't bear the sight of her. The tension in his vibrating frame sent her into a panic.

She knew that final thread of his control had unraveled, the last piece of his armor was broken. Knew that he was hurting and that he would attack at any moment. Knew what families and children and the bonds of kin would mean to his Sicilian blood.

Knew that his vulnerability, beneath the hard shell he had acquired all these years, lay in the depth and intensity with which he had once wanted love and family and laughter in his life.

Knew that he was made for it, that he would make a fantastic father. Knew that she was weakening already after facing the truth about the pregnancy, and seeing him so close by, remembering how good it had felt to give herself over to him…

He was the man she adored with every breath in her. He was the man who showed her to be strong, who showed her what she was made of.

He would fight for custody, she knew. He would do what he deemed to be right by their child. He would tie her up in clauses and contracts, he would use the fact that she hadn't instantly told him to tie her to him.

To achieve what he had wanted two months ago.

Even as every inch of her thrummed with pain, even as every inch of her recoiled at subjecting her coming child to separate parents living across the globe, Clio made her decision as the woman he had helped her become.

It was better her child had two parents who loved him, rather than a mother who would forever be in agony, living with the man who would never love her back, a mother who would so easily become a shadow of herself.

She straightened her spine and faced him. Waited for the hardest battle of her life to commence. "No. I wouldn't have hid it from you. But I…" she swallowed the tears in her throat, "I would have given myself a few weeks to prepare first."

"Prepare for what?" Stefan threw back at Clio, finding it unbearable to meet her eyes. How deep and sharp her words cut, how easily she had turned him into this mass of ache and love…

Her denial didn't bring him even infinitesimal relief. His gut still ached, his breath rushed out of him unevenly.

She would have taken a few weeks to prepare herself… that he had driven her to this, it traveled through him like a missile launched specifically to torture him.

He turned, not sure what he would say, and stilled.

With her palm splayed against her stomach, her green eyes shining with tenderness and determination, she faced him. The wide curve of her mouth trembled. It was the most beautiful sight he had ever seen and it only brought home again how much he loved this woman. How fortunate that she would mother his child…

"Please answer me, Clio. Preparing for what?" he asked again, fisting his hands at his sides, stifling the urge to take her in his arms.

She shrugged, but the casualness she was going for didn't come through. There was a wariness in her eyes that he decided he would never be the cause of again.

"I knew that if I had told you immediately, you would come armed to the teeth with clauses and contracts. That you would want this child and me and the whole family thing. That you would seduce your way into my life and convince me this was for the best. As sad as it sounds, I need to shore up my defenses against you."

"You think I will bind you to me in the name of our child? You think me that heartless, Clio?"

Tears ran over her cheeks and she swayed. Cursing himself over and over, Stefan caught her.

"What am I supposed to think, Stefan? Two months have gone by and you didn't call me once. Two months in which I wondered if I would ever see you again. Two months in which every minute felt like an eternity. Two months in which I battled the urge to come to you, to beg you to take me back any way you wanted."

He grabbed her hands, willing her to understand him. "I hurt you so much that day. I couldn't face myself in the mirror thinking of what I had ruined. The minute you had walked out, I realized what I had done, how wrong I was.

"I have been cursing myself, wondering if I could ever take back what I had done. I was terrified that I would hurt you even more after everything you have been through, Clio. I'm terrified that I might never be worthy of you, *bella*."

He knelt in front of her, wrapped his arms around her. Bent his head, burrowed into her warmth, the love he felt for her unmanning him.

And even as he trembled at the thought that he might have lost her, he could feel the rightness of this, feel everything in him slide into place. Striving for control that was out of his reach, he pulled her fingers in his hand and kissed her.

"Stefan?" she whispered. There was so much pain and hope in it that he ached.

He raised his head and met her beautiful gaze, poured the emotions flowing through him into words. "I'm desperately in love with you. With every breath in my body. With every cell in my being. I come to you today with nothing but my heart in my hands, Clio.

"All I want is to be part of your life, a chance to show you how much I adore you. Every moment of my life, every decision I have ever taken, it…it has made me into this. But it also brought me to you, *bella*.

"The bastard that I am today, I'm still all yours to do with, Clio."

Sinking to her knees, she clutched him. "Oh, Stefan…"

And just when Stefan thought he couldn't fragment anymore, that he could feel no more, the sound of her pain pierced him again.

Wrapping his arms around her gingerly, he pulled her onto his lap. Buried his face in her hair and breathed in a lungful of her scent. Pushed himself to be the man that was worthy of the generous, brave woman that his beautiful wife was.

"Please, Clio. Do not cry, *cara*. I will not challenge you over our child. I will walk out, I will sign any paper you want me to sign. All I want is your happiness, even if it will kill me to be away from you."

Meeting his gaze, she rested her forehead against his. "You really want me? Me and not just the mother of your child?"

Hating that she doubted him, hating that he had given her cause to, he hugged her to him.

"I came today because I couldn't bear to be apart from you anymore, Clio. I couldn't breathe for the thought of never seeing you smile again." His hand moved over her stomach, and his breath caught in his throat. "That you… that you carry a part of me inside you…it's more than I wished for in my wildest dreams, *bella*. Will you truly be my wife, Clio? Will you help me be the man you deserve again?"

"You're already everything I could have ever hoped for, Stefan. You know me better than anyone else in the world. And you take care of me, you enable me, you…you love me more than anyone else ever has, even as you shred me to pieces. Loving you—" tears pooled in her eyes and overflowed "—somehow, it has only made me stronger."

His heart thudded fast in his chest, the back of his eyes prickling with warmth. "I love you so much, *bella*…I have missed you so much…it felt like a part of me was forever gone. Promise you will never walk away from me, Clio. Even if I make a mistake, promise me you will fight for me."

Shaking her head, she covered his mouth with her hand. Sank her hands into his hair and tugged him up. Pressed her mouth to his and kissed him so hard and for so long that he came undone.

"All I want is my friend, my lover, my husband back, Stefan. All I want is the man who made me the best I could be. And if we make a mistake, we'll rail and rage at other, but we will always find our way to each other again."

Reaching for her mouth, Stefan breathed in her scent, clutched her to him. With Clio by his side, there would be nothing but happiness and joy in the coming days.

Combing his fingers through her hair, he kissed her forehead, a smile curving his mouth. "I want a little girl with hair the color of fire."

Turning around, Clio tucked her face under his chin, her arms tightly vined around his midriff. "Do you think we will be good parents?"

The thread of anxiety in her tone, that she would show him her fears, made his chest fill up. "We will be the best parents in the world, *bella*. If we do make any mistakes, he or she will have grandparents and a host of aunts and uncles to complain to," he said, thinking of Rocco and Christian and Zayed and the wonderful women they had married.

His heart seemed as if it was bursting to the full. Their friends would be over the moon for him, would find so much happiness in his.

"New York or Sicily?" he said, his hands roving restlessly over her lithe curves. With a moan that curled around his senses, she pushed herself into his touch.

Found his mouth with hers and demanded everything. Nipped his lower lip with her teeth until he was rock-hard under her. Splaying her legs wide around him, she rubbed herself over his erection, and let out another long moan.

"New York and Sicily, with regular stops at Milan, Athens and Gazbiyaa," she breathed, her fingers busy over his belt buckle.

The moment her fingers danced over his rigid shift, Stefan pushed her down to the carpet and covered her with his body.

This time, they both groaned, and joy filled his heart. "That should work, *bella*," he finished and kissed his wife's luscious mouth.

* * * * *

Look out for the next installment of
SOCIETY WEDDINGS:
THE SHEIKH'S WEDDING CONTRACT
by Andie Brock
Coming next month!

Read on for a SOCIETY WEDDINGS *exclusive!*

DELETED SCENE

"WHERE IS SHE, OLIVIA?"

Olivia Mondelli stared with increasing shock at the man standing on the doorstep of her Manhattan apartment, his face wearing the most unexpected expression she had ever seen.

Stefan Bianco...

That expression was a combination of fear and something she thought she would never see on one of the hardest men she had ever met.

Oh, she had seen the best of them during her career as one of the top models in New York. Playboys, charmers and models alike, but no one quite like Stefan.

The hard shell that the man had beneath that sophisticated arrogance, it was bone deep.

And yet, Liv had seen that shell rattle over the past few months as Clio had come back into his life.

Had watched in fascination as the fiercely protective side of him emerged as, to even Rocco's shock, Stefan had married Clio in a wedding that was nothing short of a fairy tale. Had seen Clio change from the pale shadow she had been at Christian's wedding into one of the strongest women Liv had ever seen.

Even more of a shocker was the genuinely contented laughter she had seen in Stefan's eyes at Zayed's wedding.

She had even held her breath for them as she had seen the obvious truth of how deeply Clio had fallen for him.

She had bet Rocco that they would make it, had believed that if anyone could shatter the hard shell that Stefan carried around, it had to be Clio.

Clio, who had become as close to her as the sister she had never had.

But, of course, Rocco had known his friend better, and had waited on tenterhooks almost for the crash that had eventually come at Zayed's wedding.

Only a few hours after the wedding, Clio had come to her, pale and trembling and yet somehow, stronger than she had ever seen before, begging to leave Gazbiyaa with Liv and Rocco, and return to New York.

That was almost two months ago.

Two months in which Clio had stayed in New York and Stefan, to Olivia's shock, had disappeared. She had seen him a couple of times traveling with Rocco and both times, he had been hungry, almost desperate for information about Clio.

Yet, he hadn't inquired once after Clio.

Today, Rocco, who was in Milan, had called her exactly two hours ago, warning her that Stefan was coming back to New York.

And here he was, glaring at her, as if it was his God-given right.

Olivia would have despised his arrogance and his irrational dislike of her when they had first met if she hadn't seen firsthand how fiercely devoted he was to Rocco and Christian and Zayed.

"Hello to you, too, Stefan," she said cheerily, opening the door wider. "It's a gorgeous New York morning, isn't it?"

He didn't even blink at her saccharine tone. Prowled inside casually with his long-limbed stride and yet, Liv could sense something restless in his calm movements, something strange.

For the first time in two months, Liv felt a flutter of hope for Clio.

"I want to see Clio, Olivia. Where is she?"

The smile disappeared from her face, an image of Clio with tears in her eyes flashing in front of her eyes.

"Does Clio know you're here, Stefan?"

The facade of politeness crumbled from his face and Olivia caught her gasp from escaping.

Vulnerability and Stefan Bianco weren't words she would have thought of in the same sentence even.

"How the hell does it matter if she knows or not, Liv?"

"Because I remember her telling me that she didn't want to see you, Stefan."

"Damn it, Liv, she's my wife, and I would like to see her. When the hell did you become her gatekeeper?"

"When I saw how broken she was after Zayed's wedding. That's when. I let down a friend once and I won't let anything to happen to her. Even though you don't realize it, Clio is—"

"*Dio*, Olivia. Clio is precious, don't you think I know that?" While Olivia stared stunned, he ran a hand over his eyes. And Liv saw past her own prejudice and noticed how tired he looked. He cleared his throat as though choosing his words carefully. "I'm so glad that you're looking out for her. But I need to see her. I need to…"

"You need to what, Stefan?"

A glimmer of a smile curved his mouth, transforming his entire face. "This wouldn't be revenge, would it, Liv? For my doubting you when you and Rocco were beginning? Because, really, you couldn't have chosen a better way to torture me."

Such warmth radiated from his green gaze that Liv felt her heart contract. This was the best friend her husband cherished so much. Finally, she saw why Rocco worried so much for Stefan, especially after Rocco and she had found each other.

This was what he and Stefan and Christian and Zayed did for each other.

Swallowing the lump in her throat, Liv smiled at him. "No. As enticing as it sounds, this is not revenge, Stefan. Clio is my friend now."

Liv met his gaze and waited. And his confession, when it came, was so hoarse and uneven.

"I love her, Olivia. I…I have insulted her, and bullied her and I…hurt her. I can't…I can't live without seeing her smile…but I have nothing to offer her."

Olivia had goose bumps on her skin, tears in her eyes. "Remember what you told me that day, Stefan?" Grabbing his hand, Liv squeezed it, dying to call Rocco and tell him.

"Those three words…that's all it takes, Stefan."

STOP THE PRESS
NEWS ARTICLE

Stefan Bianco and Clio Norwood—A Fairy Tale Too Good to Believe or a True Love Story?

In a shocking move that has left New York's finance society dropping their jaws, luxury real estate mogul Stefan Bianco, one of New York's very own illustrious Columbia Four, the man who has been dubbed One-Date Wonder by more than one scorned lover in the past, really tied the knot with Clio Norwood, the society hostess who turned her back on her illustrious family a decade ago.

The old college friends from Columbia made it official at the prestigious Chatsfield, surrounded by their close friends and the glitterati from New York's high society.

The redheaded bride shone in a designer tulle and diamonds while the groom, who had stolen her from under the nose of financier Jackson Smith, looked splendid in a black-and-white tuxedo.

"After knowing each other for more than a decade, it's so obvious that they have always belonged with each other," a friend close to the gorgeous couple shared.

Well, here's hoping that Mrs. Bianco can hold on to her title *and* the man this time.